IN HIS NAME

Samuel Uriah Goodman

A Pale Horse Media Co. Book

www.palehorsemedia.co

In His Name

Copyright © 2021 by Samuel Uriah Goodman

All rights reserved. No part of this book may be reproduced or transmitted in any form or by any means without written permission from the author.

This is a work of fiction. Names, characters, businesses, places, events, locales, and incidents are either the products of the author's imagination or used in a fictitious manner. Any resemblance to actual persons, living or dead, or actual events is purely coincidental.

ISBN 9798705871858

Published by Pale Horse Media Co.

Other Books by Sam Goodman

"Safety Sucks! The BULL $H!* in the Safety Profession They Don't Tell You About."
S. Goodman 2020

"Obscured: The Pursuit of Radical Self-acceptance."
S. Goodman 2020

Visit www.palehorsemedia.co for more

Dedication

This book is dedicated to Misty Bailey and Chy Davis. Thank you for being the best sisters a brother could ask for.

"Why are deviled eggs such a staple of these things?" Elijah Howard thought to himself as he surveyed the tables of food before him. He was at his first church potluck since arriving in town; quite the gathering for the sleepy little community of Langford, Tennessee. He had been in town for just a few short weeks at this point, making the trek up from Nashville after receiving the news about his aunt. After filling his plate, he made his way back across the crowded room and into his seat. "Can I get you anything Aunt Ruby?" Elijah asked before scooting in his chair. Aunt Ruby replied with silence; emitting a brief smile and shake of her head. The near-ancient metal folding chair groaned and screamed as Elijah pulled himself into the table. Everyone seemed to turn and glance at him before turning back to their little groups; they all gave him a curious looking over before returning to their roaring conversations. Elijah did not fit in, he stood out like a sore thumb in Langford.

From his head to his feet Elijah Howard screamed "city boy." Though one should not judge a book by its cover, his appearance could be deceiving. As of late, Nashville had been his home. But he grew up in a small town not much different than the one he found himself in now. He had a fairly normal upbringing in a small rural area of South Carolina. He was not the best or the worst student; he graduated dead middle of his high school class. He played some sports, he had a few friends, and was wildly normal in most regards. He spent a few years in college, earned half of a degree, and then ran away to Nashville for work, culture, and the offerings a better life. Nashville offered opportunity his rural home could not. Even though he was now a city slicker, he remained a country boy at heart. Elijah was a mixture of two very different worlds; he could tell you the best skin care routine for men and also start a fire with his bare hands and a few sticks. As much as he stood out in Langford, he seemed to mostly blend in elsewhere in his life.

Elijah was not tall or short, he was not skinny or fat, he was not muscular or flabby. Elijah was a pretty normal man in most regards. One thing did stand out about Elijah, his striking attractiveness. His well-kept dark hair, the way that he carried himself, and his glowing smile, drew the attention of many, many onlookers. But Elijah was perpetually single; he seemed uninterested in the notions of courtship. He did not flirt, and he did not date. Many women vied for his attention and never received it. Langford was no different, Elijah was a desirable bachelor in this small town. He was a big fish in a small pond; Elijah was fresh meat. Even as he sat next to his ailing Aunt Ruby, the flirtatious stares would not stop. It seemed that every woman between the ages of 18 and dead, had their eyes on Elijah. Many people gazed lustfully at him; just as many looked at him distrustfully as an outsider. Either way, Elijah did not fit in in Langford, Tennessee.

A couple of weeks ago, Elijah was still in Nashville. He was going about his normal life, a mixture of work and friends. He had really carved out his own little existence in the big city. He landed a good job working as a human resources specialist for a small company, he had grown a small and tight group of friends, and he had recently leased his dream loft in downtown. He had come a long way from his humble upbringing's in that small South Carolina town. He had just gotten to the point of creating a real existence in Nashville when his life was suddenly interrupted. As he was wrapping up at work one evening, his phone rang. Its noisy mixture of ringing and vibrating startled him for a few brief moments. He stood up quickly from his office chair, digging through his pockets for the culprit. Finally retrieving the phone from his back pocket, he could see that it was his mom. "She's still at work, why is she calling me now?" Elijah muttered to himself. Realizing that it must be important, he answered. "Hey mom, what up?" he said as he accepted the call. "Hey honey, I'm just here at work. I actually just got off the phone with your Aunt Ruby," she said as she responded to him. She continued on, "Your Aunt Ruby isn't doing well, the doctors say that she only has a few months left."

Near the beginning of the year, Aunt Ruby had been diagnosed with cancer. Ruby was an avid smoker and had been one for as long as anyone could remember. She loved Jesus, menthol cigarettes, and cheesecake, more than anything in this world. That order was subject to change based on the type of day she was having. After putting off going to the doctor for months, she finally gave in. She could now sense her rapid decline and knew that she needed help. She traveled a few towns over to the bustling metropolitan area of Lola, Tennessee. Lola is about triple the size of Langford; it is the county seat. Being the county seat, it provides the full gamut of county services: The Water & Power Department, the Watkins County Sheriff's Office, a district courthouse, a Tennessee State Police substation, and a slew of other staple institutions. It is also home to the only real hospital for 100 miles or so, a few chain restaurants, a shopping mall leftover from the early 1990's, and a couple of car dealerships. Lola felt normal; Lola was a pleasant little town. This quaint little township would be the backdrop for some of the worst news that an individual can receive. After a gamut of pokes, prods, and tests at The Lola Regional Medical Center, Aunt Ruby knew the truth. She was diagnosed with stage IV non-small cell lung cancer. Aunt Ruby would soon be dead.

"Elijah, I need you go to Langford." his mother said through the phone. "I know that you don't know Ruby that well, but she's my sister, she's your aunt, and the family needs you to do this." she added. "I – I – I'm," Elijah stuttered as he tried to formulate a response. "You're the closest to her, the rest of the family is scattered across the country, honey. It'll just be for a few weeks or so." His mother said. "I've never even been to Langford and what am I supposed to do about work?" Elijah responded. "It's just a few weeks, she needs help for the last few weeks of her life Elijah. When things worsen, the rest of the family can make it out, and you can go. We just need you to help her in the meantime, son." she responded. Elijah clacked and clicked away at his computers to find out how much paid time off he had accrued over the last year; amazingly he had just under three weeks. After a few minutes of tense and awkward silence, Elijah replied, "Mom, let me talk to my boss and I'll see what I can do."

Elijah had a reputation as a good man. He had always been known as a hard worker and an honest person. He's the type of man that people would refer to as "being raised right" or as "honest to a fault." He carried these traits with him from South Carolina to Nashville; they were on full display at his workplace. They had earned him much respect and leeway with his superiors, freedom that Elijah had never used. But he was now on his way to ask for a favor. His feet made muffled thumps as he walked down the grey carpeted hallway towards his boss's office. He walked slowly; a journey to Langford was not what Elijah wanted. He half-hoped that his boss would deny his request and sentence him to some dreadful work project instead. He walked slowly down the hall, hopeful that something would change before he made his request. "Maybe she'll die before I have to go?" he thought for a brief moment before reeling in shame from his morbid fantasy. Langford was not part of his plan; he would rather stay home in Nashville. But Elijah could not say "no;" he could not risk disappointing his mother. He lightly knocked on the tall oak door and awaited permission to enter. Near instantly his boss shouted, "come on in!" The large door felt heavy as Elijah pushed against it; it emitted a loud groaning noise as he pushed it open. Behind a dated cherrywood desk set Bill Porter, HR manager for HRK Inc. "Elijah! How are you doing today? What can I do you for?" Bill excitedly said. Mr. Porter was a short and round little man with a glowing red face. He always seemed to have just finished running a flight of steps; he was often red, sweaty, and out of breath. Mr. Porter was always happy; he loved his life, and he loved his job. Bill Porter was good man and a good boss.

After some back and forth of your typical meaningless office conversation, Elijah made the ask. "My Aunt Ruby Morgan lives up in Langford, and unfortunately she's pretty sick with cancer." Elijah began to explain to Mr. Porter. "It sounds like she only has a few weeks left and my mom has asked if I can head up and help her out," Elijah continued. Bill's happy and glowing red face was overcome with concern. Bill knew the perils of cancer; his mother had died from the disease years prior. "I'm not awfully close with her, but I would be doing my family a huge favor. I'll completely understand if it's a no Mr. Porter," Elijah said. "Family first Elijah!" Bill said dutifully. "Go! Take some time. You have plenty of PTO. If you need more time beyond that, we'll figure it out. But I mean this, family first!" he added. "Thank you for this Mr. Porter," Elijah replied. "How many times do I have to tell you Elijah? It's Bill! Mr. Porter was my dad!" he said lightheartedly.

It was all now set-in motion; Elijah would go to Langford. He walked defeatedly back towards his desk with his head down. He did not want to spend the next few weeks in rural Tennessee; anything rural now seemed like a hellscape to him. But Elijah was too nice to say no and wanted to do right by his aunt. He would soon trade his bustling metropolitan life for one that moved at the speed of molasses. He had a few work projects he needed to wrap up and he wanted to see some friends before he left; he would depart in a few days. He hoped to soak up as much of the city as could; maybe he could carry some of it with him to Langford. He sent a text to his mother, "I'll head up before the end of the week. Please let Aunt Ruby know that I'll be there Saturday night." He followed up that text message with another, though this was to a group message of his closest friends. "Let's all meet up for a drink after work?" Elijah asked the group. His phone almost instantly came to life in his hands with their replies of "yes!" and "best idea you've had in a while!"

"Just use it as a vacation!" Brit said. Brittany "Brit" Platts had been one of Elijah's best friends since he first moved to Nashville. They had discovered each other while doing laundry in their old apartment complex. They hand been drawn to each other, and bonded over, Brits *Black Flag* t-shirt. Brit and Elijah were closest of friends. "I second that! It'll be like camping but less fun," Tristan laughed. Tristan Rivera is the closest thing to a brother that Elijah has. Originally meeting through Brit, Tristan and Elijah grown a deep bond and friendship of their own. Hunter Howell remained silent sipping his beer; all eyes turned to him for his opinion. Hunter and Elijah had met at the Gym a few months after Elijah's move to the big city. He has always been more of the shy and quiet type, but always has deep and insightful commentary. "I don't know why the fuck everyone is laughing about it; his aunt is dying!" Hunter spouted off. "Jesus Christ grow up y'all!" he the said irritably. "You're right!" Elijah replied. He slid around the slippery leather booth and put his arm around Hunter. "You all are right!" he said. "I'm going to take care of my aunt. But I'm going to look on the bright side and take this time away to relax and get away from it all," Elijah concluded. Everyone shook their heads in silent agreement with Elijah's statement. "But you losers are coming to visit," he said. "Give me a couple few weeks to get settled in, then come up for a long weekend?" he added. Brit quickly responded with a loud "Hell yes! Road trip!" Tristan simply smiled in agreement, and Hunter rolled his eye indicating a strong "maybe."

  The weekly potluck at The Second Coming Bible Church was a far cry from that swank and hip bar Elijah had found himself in just a few short weeks prior. Instead of sipping craft tequila and eating crispy pork belly, Elijah now sipped off-brand cola and munched on deviled eggs. A short, very round, and wrinkled old women started to make her way towards the table at which Aunt Ruby and Elijah set. Elijah watched her fluffy permed snow-white hair bounce through the crowd of people; it looked like a ball of cotton he thought. After pausing to say hello to few groups of friends, she eventually made her way to Aunt Ruby. "Ruby, how are you? How are you feeling? I've been praying for you." the old woman said. "I'm alive thanks be to God," Ruby said hoarsely. "Now that I have a little help around the house, things are that much better," Ruby continued. "We haven't met yet," the old woman said with deep southern drawl aimed in Elijah's direction. "I'm Granny Jean Ward," she said introducing herself. "It's nice to meet you Mrs. Ward, I'm Elijah Howard. I am Ruby's nephew," Elijah politely and properly replied. "Now, now, don't start with that Mrs. Ward stuff. Most just call me granny around these parts," she replied. "Granny, pastor needs you," someone shouted from across the noisy fellowship hall. "Duty calls," Granny muttered as she departed the table. Her little cotton ball swath of white hair disappearing into the crowd as she made her way to find the pastor.

"So, who is she?" Elijah inquisitively asked his aunt. "She's been here since forever; Granny was a founding member of this church." Aunt Ruby explained. "I think she even came up with name," she continued. "The Second Coming Bible Church is not something I would brag about," Elijah thought to himself and chuckled softly. His humorous moment was cut short by a loud and deep rumbling voice, "Everyone, everyone, let's turn down the volume just a notch. I need to cover the announcements and then I'll get out of your hair," said a man from across the room. Elijah was scanning the crowd, trying to find the source of the words. The crowd started to part; people swiftly moved against the walls to make room. A man emerged from the parting sea of people, an old man in a dark colored suit. Aunt Ruby leaned over and whispered in Elijah's ear, "that's pastor Jacob Eldridge and the blonde lady beside of him is his wife Carrol." Elijah nodded with understanding. This entire potluck experience was reminding him why he had so carefully avoided attending church with Aunt Ruby in the first place. But she had begged him to come, and he finally gave in to the wishes of a dying woman.

"We have Sunday School in the morning followed directly by our normal Sunday service, Tuesday night we have an elders and deacons meeting, Wednesday we have praise and worship service followed by a sermon, Thursday is choir practice, and Friday we will gather for more fellowship." Pastor Eldridge rattled off from a scrap of paper in his hand. "Let me leave you with the word of God before I finally leave you with the food," the pastor said with a slight chuckle. "I told you that you would die in your sins; if you do not believe that I am he, you will indeed die in your sins – John 8:24. Don't die in your sins brothers and sisters. Repent before God and repent before your church! Amen!" Pastor Eldridge said while raising his hand towards the ceiling. A random "amen" echoed from the crowd, followed by a "preach pastor!" "I look forward to seeing each and every one of you at church in the morning. Have a great remainder of your night." Pastor Eldridge concluded with a quick wave to the crowd. He then disappeared into his flock; Elijah lost sight of him as he shook hands while moving through the congregation.

Elijah peered up at the black and white clock on the wall, the old bland type of clock that's design has never changed. He emitted an audible sigh; time seemed to somehow move slower in Langford, Tennessee. "How long are we staying?" Elijah asked Ruby. "Oh, just long enough to get to visit. I'm taking it all in while I can," she replied. Elijah slumped over in that old beige metal chair and rested his face in his hands; people watching to kill the time. He remained in this position for what seemed like hours, watching people come and go from the buffet of food. His wrist was sore from shaking hands; each introduction seemed like a test of his grip strength. Person after person made their way by the table to check on Ruby and to formally introduce themselves. Elijah had already grown bored of their repetitious questions; he found himself annoyed by Aunt Ruby's repetitious responses. They all seemed to ask the same things: "How are you Ruby? How do you feel? We're here for you!" It all just seemed like meaningless bull shit. Ruby would offer the same generic reply that she had offered hundreds of times prior, "I'm alive thanks be to God. I'm doing a lot better now that Elijah is here to help." Elijah had long since grown tired of this theater, but he would continue to play along for as long Aunt Ruby wanted to stay.

There are just certain people that carry themselves differently; some people stand out even when they blend in. As Elijah's boredom and frustration grew, he continued people watching to help pass the time. As he examined the room, moving from person to person, most seemed to blend in. People of this particular sect of Christianity seem to have a certain look about them. They are modestly dressed, lacking of makeup or other "worldly" things, and somehow seem to emit their faith from every cell of their bodies. Everyone in this room shared those characteristics; but some stood out from the herd. "Who are those folks at the front table?" Elijah asked of his aunt. "Those are the church deacons. Susan Phillips, Rebecca Stevens, Elizabeth Johns, and Benjamin Johns," Aunt Ruby said. "Poor Susan and Rebecca are widowers; their husbands died years ago. Elizabeth and Benjamin are married and serve together. They help Pastor Eldridge lead the church," Ruby continued. At the end of the deacons table set a large-framed, rough looking middle-aged man. His head was shiny and bald; he did not have the same jovial look as most of the congregation. The man looked as if he had seen things, like he was "shell-shocked." He set there never touching his food, only staring blankly at the wall in front of him. "What about him?" Elijah inquired while motioning in the man's direction with a nod. "Oh, that's Randall Ward, he's Granny Jean's grandson. Well, adoptive son I guess, but he's always just called her granny," Ruby replied. "They found him down at the old fire station, that poor thing. Someone just abandoned him there," Ruby said in a concerned tone. "But Granny raised him right! He works for the county and is pastors' right-hand man," she concluded.

Some people stand out even when they blend in; the wolves stood out from the sheep. Randy Ward was a wolf, you could just see it. Those in power stood out; they stood out worse than Elijah against this backdrop. "What is the deal?" Elijah thought to himself while pondering the congregation's social intricacies. His astute observations, those made while people watching, revealed clear lines within the crowd. People seemed grouped by rank and title; everyone had a place and seemed to know exactly where that place was. As he scanned the room, more and more wolves seemed to stand out. The fellowship hall had a front and back entrance; there were men stationed next to each. These men all had the same traumatic look etched upon their faces; the same look Elijah had originally noticed on Randy Ward. The more Elijah looked, the more he could see. Even at the table he found himself at; Aunt Ruby was slightly pulled away from the group. It was like she was on display, like he was on display. He continued to peer around the crowded fellowship hall trying to make sense of what he was looking at.

With a loud metallic screech, Aunt Ruby stood up from the table. The old-style metal folding chairs made a hideous noise against the aged tile floors. "Well Elijah, I guess that's enough for tonight," She said. "I'm tired and need some rest if I'm going to be of any use at tomorrows service!" she concluded. Elijah snapped out of his fever-dream with an audible gasp; the loud noise had startled him. "Yeah, of course! Let's get you home Aunt Ruby," he replied to her while shaking off his fright. Elijah hurriedly picked up the flimsy foam plates and cups from the table; he cleaned and cleared the mess as fast as he could. He had constructed a mound of Styrofoam dinnerware in his arms. With one hand supporting the bottom, and the other compressing the top of this trash tower, he rushed towards the garbage can in the corner of the room. Elijah did not want to risk Aunt Ruby changing her mind, he was more than ready to go. As fast as he had started moving, he came to an even faster stop. "What is that?" Elijah thought to himself as he stared at this long, cylindrical, and bright tube flickering tube above him. He couldn't seem to make sense as to what exactly he was looking at. A dark object eclipsed the light and slowly came into focus; it was a face.

"Goodness! Are you ok?" the deep male voice inquired. "Wh, wh, wha, what happened?" Elijah said stuttering in his response. "Well, I think someone spilled some coffee and you found it," the unknown person said laughingly. "You took quite the tumble! Let me help you up?" the man asked while extending a hand. Elijah grasped it and was tugged up from the floor. "Damn, I mean dang, that hurt!" Elijah said while shaking off the fall. "I'm Seth Nelson, it's nice to meet you. Your Aunt Ruby has told us all about you," he said. "It's nice to meet you Seth, though I wish it were under different circumstances," Elijah replied still reeling from the fall. "It looks like someone is ready to go," Seth said while motioning towards Aunt Ruby. "Yeah, I better get going, it was nice to meet you.

Thanks again for the help," Elijah replied. "No problem! Hey, let's hangout sometime? You're new here, I'm bored, it could be fun?" Seth purposed. "Yeah, that might work," Elijah replied while digging for his phone. "Let me give you my num…" he started to say before Seth cut him off. "No need, I'll just call Ruby's! Nice meeting you Elijah," Seth said as he started walking away. Elijah collected his wits and made his way towards Aunt Ruby. "That Seth is a nice boy, you two should be friends," Aunt Ruby said as Elijah resumed his place at her side. "As for you, you need to be more careful! I'm the one that's supposed to die not you!" she said in a firm motherly tone. Elijah shook his head and smirked. "Yes ma'am," he replied.

Seven traffic signals, three banks, four gas stations, a half-empty strip mall, a grocery store, a few places to eat, two churches, and some random cows dotting the surrounding green fields. Population: 1,322 souls and declining. Langford would meet the definition of "small town" by anyone's standards; some would refer to it as near microscopic. Elijah felt far-removed from his crowded existence in Nashville. Langford and Nashville seemed to exist on two distinctly separate planets; they were two vastly different and separate planes of existence. Elijah was raised in a small town; he knew rural life well. But Langford was sparce, even by his experience. The once booming agricultural epicenter of northwest Tennessee had long since ceased being productive. All that remained of hundreds of years of hard labor were some rotting tobacco barns and some pieces of rustic farming equipment; rust riddled skeletons of a once fruitful past now stood like monuments to a better time. The endless fields that once contained cotton and tobacco now set empty; with their disappearance also left the means to make ends meet in Langford. When farming left town, a choice had to be made to flee or starve. Many families undertook the great exodus from Lanford, heading north in pursuit of factory jobs and a better life. The once bustling little town now set half boarded up, a ghost of its former self.

Langford is nestled in the heart of the dense Chiaha national forest. The small community is located in the flatlands near the Kentucky and Tennessee border. To the east is Nashville, a dull three-hour drive through abandoned farmland and shelled out towns similar to Langford. Elijah knew this drive all too well, he had followed this long and boring road during his original journey to town. To the west is Langford's nearest neighbor, Lola, Tennessee. Langford is part of the Lola metropolitan area, with Lola being home to around 4,000 Tennesseans. To the north is a slew of trees and Kentuckians; to the west is the city of Jackson. Surrounding the tiny little town is a picturesque landscape of dense trees, wildlife, streams, rivers, and a large lake. In more recent years, a small park was constructed near the lakes shore. "Lakeview Park" as it was so originally named, had now become a nighttime gathering spot for the few teenagers in town, lovebirds, and the occasional junkie. During the daylight hours the park would be used for more wholesome activities; gatherings that did not require the cover of darkness. Church cookouts, baptisms in the lake, and the occasional group of small children and parents using the playground, are all common sights at Lakeview Park. Besides a drive out to Lakeview, an hour-long trip to Lola, or a journey to one of the larger surrounding cities, there was not much to see or do in Langford. The towns old movie theater had gone out of business in the 1970's, there was no shopping to speak of, and town events were few and far between. Two institutions are at the heart of most social gatherings in Langford: The Second Coming Bible Church or The Christ Almighty Worship Center. In a town devoid of work or leisure, Jesus had filled the vacuum. Elijah had already been introduced to one these town staples; he would soon meet the other. In Langford, it's only a matter of time until God finds you.

Elijah knew small town life; he knew God just as well. Before his big move to Nashville, he was born and raised in Big Rock, South Carolina. Big Rock was small, but Columbia was its saving grace. A short half-hour trip by car, and Elijah was surrounded by urban adventure. Compared to Langford, Big Rock was a city in its own right. Elijah never imagined finding himself in a place smaller than his hometown; he now looked back with admiration for his childhood home. He longed to be anywhere but Langford, even if that meant Big Rock. Elijah had a pretty normal and happy upbringing; Big Rock was pleasant little place to grow up. He was raised by his mom Victoria; his dad had died in a work accident long before he could remember him. Victoria Howard worked hard to give her son a good life; they were not rich but had plenty. She did her best to raise him in church and to instill in him the teachings of Christianity. Elijah dutifully listened to his mother; finding himself in church a few days out of each week. But Elijah and God never quite seemed to click. To this day he considers himself more a of a non-believer than anything else. With or without God, Victoria Howard raised a good kid. Elijah played varsity football, had a close-knit group of friends, and was what most would describe as an oddly quiet "jock." He was a popular person in school, though he never seemed to believe it or act the part of the popular jock. If you asked anyone at Big Rock High about Elijah, they would all respond with the same answer: "He's a good guy." Elijah graduated Big Rock High School in 2007. He then finished half of a degree at a community college in Columbia before growing bored and running away to Nashville. Elijah, now in his mid-thirties, had built a good life for himself in Nashville. A good life that he was keen on returning to sooner than later.

    As much as Elijah himself stood out in Langford, his car stood out that much more. Most residents of Langford hadn't seen a Toyota, much less a Lexus. Elijah was doing well in his career and had recently gifted himself the vehicle. "Does anyone actually live here," Elijah thought aloud as he slowly cruised through downtown Langford. He had just left Aunt Ruby's and was on his way to meet Seth Nelson. After Seth rescued him from his near-death slip at the church potluck, the two had planned to hang out. Earlier in the day, Elijah had received a text message from an unknown number: "Hey Buddy! Let's get into something?" Elijah was weary of the sender; it had been a long while since he had given his number to anyone new. Curiosity and a healthy dose of boredom got the better of him, "Who is this?" he replied a few minutes later. Near instantly there was a response, "It's Seth! Duh!" the response read. Elijah shook his head with confusion; he had not given Seth his number. His phone again vibrated to life with another message, "Before you ask, Ruby gave me your number." Slightly relieved yet still frazzled, Elijah started to type a response. With a sharp "Bzzzzzz," there was another message from Seth. "Meet me at Lakeview in an hour?" his message read. Elijah finally got a word in, "Ok, I'll be there," he replied. Seth was odd in the stereotypical small-town nice way; Elijah was desperate for human interaction and was willing to live with Seth's unique mannerisms. It had been weeks since he experienced anything remotely resembling a social life; last hanging out with his friend in one of his swank downtown Nashville haunts. Since his arrival, he had been on a steady routine of spending time with Ruby, an occasional grocery run, and avoiding going to church like it was the plague. His days mostly consisted of channel surfing Ruby's television or taking the occasional jog around town.

Ruby lived in the old Morgan homestead; Elijah's ancestors had built the home long before Langford was even Langford. His great-grandparents, his grandparents, and now his Aunt ruby lived within its walls. The small and modest home set right outside of town; a mere 15-minute jog to the town square. Elijah often used the dilapidated old gazebo of the town square as a turning back point for his jogs. On more occasions than he could now count, Elijah would run. His few short weeks of life in Lanford were already wearing on him, he used the shorts runs as an opportunity to clear his head. A 30-minute chunk of his day in which he did not have to think about Ruby, Langford, or miss his life back in Nashville. At the point of Seth's message, Elijah had hit an all-time low; he was either on the couch or running. His life had devolved into this state of stasis. Elijah was depressed and bored; he would take whatever human interaction he could get.

The small car rattled and shook loudly as Elijah hit a group of potholes while entering the parking lot of Lakeview. "Ah, fuck!" Elijah shouted loudly after the strike. There seemed to be more potholes than people in Langford; Elijah seemed to find all of them with his new car. Peering across the barren lot, he spotted an older model pickup truck. "That must be it," Elijah thought to himself as he examined the rust speckled white Ford. He slowly pulled into the adjacent space; cautiously investigating the trucks occupant. Looking up and through his passenger side window, Elijah found a familiar face awaiting him. Seth sprang to life upon the realization that Elijah had arrived, waving with one arm, and rolling down the old crank window with the other. "What's up? I'm so glad you came!" Elijah could softly hear through his window. He rushed to roll down the glass to hear Seth; his muffled words instantly became louder. "Hey, how are you?" Seth inquired. "I'm doing ok. I'm glad to get out of the house, but pretty bummed about hitting those potholes back there." Elijah said wile exiting his still running car to examine it for damage. Elijah kneeled down for a closer inspection of his rims and tires. "Yeah, I think those have been there since they built this place," Seth shouted across the car as he turned off his truck and leapt down from the driver's seat. "It looks like it's just mud, I don't see any damage," Elijah said with a sigh of relief. This car meant a lot to him, it was a symbol of his hard-earned success.

"Nothing a little soap and water can't fix," Elijah heard from above him. He turned and looked up to find Seth standing directly behind him; the bright sun outlining his silhouette. Elijah stood to meet him, his head coming to a stop at Seth's chest. Seth was much taller than Elijah remembered. Looking up to Seth's face, Elijah extended his hand for a handshake. "It's good to see you again," Elijah said. Seth threw his arms around Elijah and squeezed, "we don't shake hands in these parts," Seth said while grabbing Elijah tightly. As abrupt and odd as the embrace was, Elijah kind of enjoyed it. It had been so long since he had physical contact with another person around his age; last hugging his friends in Nashville goodbye. Seth smelled of a fresh shower and deodorant, this clean smell flooded Elijah's nostrils. He could feel the strength in Seth's arms as he pulled him closer, squeezing him hard. "It's good to see you," Seth exclaimed. "Now, hop in and let me give you your official Langford tour!" he said with excitement.

Elijah rummaged through the center console of his car for his wallet; it suddenly struck him that he had not needed it for weeks. There had been nothing to spend money on in Langford. He forced the thin billfold into the front pocket of his tight jeans, he shutoff the still running car, and locked the doors with the key fob. The car acknowledged him by emitting a sharp "click" followed by a loud "honk." He shoved his keys in his pocket, and then followed Seth around to his truck. Seth hopped in first, reaching across the long leather bench seat to unlock the passenger side door. Elijah opened the door by pulling on the pitted chrome door handle, a small grab bar overhead assisted Elijah up and into the cab. He bounced and slid across the old springy seat as he leapt into the truck, catching himself before colliding with Seth. The old white and rust colored ford smelled of aged leather and coffee; Seth's cologne blended well with its bouquet. The engine whined and cranked for several suspenseful rotations before the old truck finally sprang to life. The smell of gasoline flooded the cabin, adding a new layer to the unique fragrance of the vehicle. The old Ford jumped and shook as Seth pulled down on the shifter. The truck rumbled loudly as he pressed down on the accelerator to reverse out of the parking space. Elijah braced himself to keep from again sliding across the slick leather seat as Seth cut the steering wheel hard. The brakes emitted a sharp high-pitched noise, and the beast came to a stop; the truck again bounced and jumped as Seth tugged downward on the gearshift. Then suddenly, with a loud and rumbling "vroom," they were off to explore Langford.

The trees grew up and over the road, tangling and intertwining in a thick canopy above. They formed a dense and nearly impenetrable layer between the ground and sky. It was like driving through a dark green tunnel; random bursts of sunlight would break through small gaps and flash in Elijah's face. As foreign as these winding tree-covered country backroads felt, they made Elijah that much more homesick for Nashville. The sharp bursts of sunlight breaking through the trees reminded him of similar experiences in downtown; bright beams of sunlight finding their way through the skyscrapers and blinding him with their light. Though two completely separate worlds, they shared certain similarities.

The old truck roared and clanked its ways around the long rolling curves; loud creaks and moans were like a version of automotive death-rattle. "Don't let her scare you, she's old but she's nowhere near dead," Seth said with a grin. Elijah nervously chuckled as he gripped the shoulder belt tightly. The cab went from dark to filled with light near instantly; Elijah could feel the suns warmth begin to fill the truck. He squinted and rubbed his eyes as they adjusted to the light. "There she is!" Seth said as he pointed through the windshield. "There is the big city of Langford," he concluded. Elijah could finally see clearly enough to recognize the country hellscape that he had been trapped in, they were heading straight for it. Seth had brough him a backway from the lake; the backroads had been a place that he had yet to venture. Elijah knew Langford proper quite well but was unfamiliar with practically everything else. The truck shook as Seth pressed lightly on the brakes, slowing to the towns modest speed limit. "You hungry yet?" Seth asked in his very Southern, yet attractive tone. After a brief pause, Elijah responded, "Yeah, I could eat something." "Perfect! Let me show you around a bit and then we can swing by King Kong's Kones for a snack?" Seth said. "Perfect," Elijah replied.

"That's the old bank on the right; across the street is the new bank they built a few years back," Seth said while pointing out the corresponding buildings. "Now we're passing the best gas station in town, The Speedy Spot. They always have the best gas prices in Langford," he continued. Elijah set silently nodding his head in the passenger seat. Oddly enough, he was actually enjoying himself. Langford was awful, but he was enjoying his time with Seth. Elijah hung off of every word; Seth's deep southern accent seemed to lure him in like a snake charmers' song. "Elijah! Hey buddy, are you with me?" Seth shouted with a laugh. "You seemed to zone out there for a minute. We definitely need to get you some food soon," Seth said. A startled and now red-faced Elijah snapped to attention. "S, s, s, sorry about that. I must have dozed off there for a second," he replied. "Am I that boring?" Seth inquired in a concerned tone. Seth was anything but boring to Elijah. Before he could reply Seth burst out into laughter, "I'm kidding! Me? Boring? I think not!" Seth said as he continued to chuckle. "Just a few more sights to see and then we'll get you fed," Seth concluded.

"You should know this one, here is the church," Seth said while pointing out of the driver's side window towards The Second Coming Bible Church. "Over there is the strip mall. It has a few things still open," he continued as he leaned over to point out of Elijah's window. Elijah could again smell that clean masculine smell of Seth as he moved back towards the driver's side of the old truck. As Elijah again forced himself to snap out of the Seth's charm, he noticed a large white non-descript building ahead. For whatever reason, he had never noticed this particular building before. It looked like it had once been a garage or warehouse, but now it bore a large black cross painted on the door along with a sign Elijah could not make out due to the distance. "Wait, what about that?" Elijah said while pointing towards the large white metal building. "Oh, that's the other church. Well at least that's what they call themselves," Seth said as he answered Elijah's question. Elijah's puzzled look indicated that he was not satisfied with Seth's answer. Sensing Elijah's growing curiosity, Seth continued. "That is the Christ Almighty Worship Center," Seth explained. "They don't really believe the way that we believe at the church," he continued. Elijah's confusion continued to make itself known on his face. "Umm... They are new school, and the church is more old school. We follow the bible as God's law, and they get a little looser with it," Seth said. Elijah could sense Seth's sensitivity to the topic; now was not the time pry deeper. He was enjoying Seth's company and didn't want to stir up any ill feelings; he placed is curiosity on hold. "Oh, ok. How about that food?" Elijah said. "I thought you'd never ask!" Seth exclaimed as he grabbed Elijah by the shoulder. He could feel a near electricity in his touch; Elijah's lack of human contact was getting the better of him.

A light metallic jingle greeted Seth and Elijah as they pulled open the door and made their way into the restaurant. The small and narrow dining room smelled of bleach, coffee, and food cooking in the kitchen; this mixture remined Elijah of his hospital visits with Aunt Ruby. He was near instantly transported in his mind to Lola Regional Medical Center by the smell. "Booth or table?" the hostess inquired. Seth and Elijah stared blankly at each other. "Booth it is," the hostess replied with an answer to her own question. The slippery and bouncy old seats of the booth reminded Elijah of the old white and rust speckled ford waiting the parking lot. He bounced and slid trying to take his seat. "What's good here?" Elijah asked Seth. "The hotdogs are amazing, you can't go wrong with the peach milkshake, and pretty much everything else is awful," Seth said with chuckle. King Kong's Kones is a staple of Langford, Tennessee and has been continuously operating since 1953. Serving up the best southern style hotdogs and old-fashioned custard around; people come from miles for a quick treat. Elijah laughed and snorted at Seth's answer; Seth satisfaction with finally cracking Elijah's shell was apparent in his smirking grin. "Hot dogs and custard it is," Elijah said while trying to contain his laughter.

The laughter quickly fell into silence; the awkward lull between ordering and being served was in full effect. Seth broke the silence, "First date jitters?" he asked. Elijah froze; every bit of color fled his skin and his eyes widened. "I'm just kidding Eli!" Seth said with a nervous laugh. Elijah felt like he was a kid again; flashbacks to his youth in South Carolina crossed his mind. That was last time anyone had called him Eli, the last time he feared being "outed," and it was the last time he had experienced that type of first date panic. Shaking off the experience, Elijah joined in the laughter with Seth. "So, what's the city like?" Seth asked. "I've been to Nashville once on a field trip, but that was years ago," he continued. Elijah paused for a moment; he racked his brain for a "best of" list to share with Seth but fell short of the task. "Well, the city just has a lot to offer. There is amazing food, places, people, and music." Elijah replied. "It's the mixture of everything; I guess I would say it's the culture," he concluded. Seth remined silent as he reflected on what Elijah had shared. Elijah then asked the same of Seth, "What's it like living here? I grew up in a rural town, but nothing like this." Seth again chuckled and replied, "My answers pretty much the same as yours minus the music; It is all about the food, places, and people."

"Two hots dogs, one peach shake, and one strawberry shake," the waitress said as she neared the table. "Peach shake goes over here," Elijah replied. The waitress smiled in Elijah's direction and set the heavy shake and hotdog down in front of him with a dull thud. "Anything else I can get y'all?" she inquired. "I think we're ok." Elijah replied politely. "I bet you can't get culture or food like this in Nashville," Seth said laughingly as he dug into his food. "I bet you're right," Elijah replied as he followed suit. Silence again fell over the table as the couple started to eat. They were both much hungrier than they had thought; there was barely enough room to breathe between bites much less chit chat. The food far exceeded Elijah assumptions. It was only a hotdog and milkshake, but it was the best hotdog and milkshake he had ever had. About halfway through the meal, with his belly now nearly full, Elijah restarted the conversation. His discussion with Seth about life in Nashville had got him thinking; he was growing to like Seth and wanted to get to know him better. "Let me show it to you," he said abruptly. "Show me what?" Seth asked with a puzzled look. "Nashville, let me take you one day?" Elijah asked. "We can drive up on a Friday night and stay the weekend at my place. What do you think?" he continued. The question seemed to catch Seth off guard; Lola had been the farthest he had traveled in quite some time. Sensing his nervousness with the proposition Elijah firmly said, "Just say yes." He continued on, "you'll love it! You've given me this amazing tour and treated me to a great meal, the least I can do it return the favor." Elijah scooted up on the edge of the springy booth seat; rhythmically drumming the table with his fingers in anticipation of Seth's answer. "Fine! I can't say no to that," Seth said after his short stint of silence. "That settles it," Elijah then said.

"Anything else I can get you boys?" the waitress asked as she lightly tapped the table with her long red acrylic nails. After staring blankly at one another for a few moments, Seth finally replied, "I think we are ok, thank you." "Well, here's the check, I can ring you up at the counter when you're ready. Take your time," she said. "So, you're heading to Nashville?" a deep and coarse voice inquired from behind Elijah. He quickly turned to see who was there; this small-town intrusion was not something that Elijah was accustomed to. A police officer in a dark brown uniform was sitting with his back to him; directly in front of the officer was an older man in a dark suite complete with a bright red necktie. "Hey Pastor Hall! Hey Sherriff Morales! I didn't see y'all come in," Seth said while peering around a confused Elijah. "Yeah, Elijah here is going to show me the big city," Seth continued. "Elijah, meet pastor Bill Hall. He's the pastor over at Christ Almighty, the church you were asking about earlier. This is Sheriff Jackson Morales, he comes to us by way of Tucson, Arizona. How long have you been here now Sherriff?" Seth said. "A little over a year now, it's hard to believe. It's nice to meet you Elijah," Sheriff Morales replied. "It's nice to meet you Sherriff Morales and Pastor Hall" Elijah said. Sherriff Morales nodded in acknowledgement. "It's nice to meet you son, just call me Pastor Bill" the old man replied from across the table. "You we're asking about the church? You should come by and join us for a service. We'd love to have you," Pastor Bill said with a smile. "Well Jackson, let's not pester these two fine young men any more than we already have," Pastor Bill said while scooting his way out of the slippery booth seat. "You boys have a fine afternoon and God bless," he said with a slight wave while walking past the table. "Boys," Sherriff Morales said with a nod while following the pastor towards the register.

"You're getting to meet all of the town bigwigs today," Seth said with a sarcastic chuckle. "Yeah, they seemed pretty nice actually," Elijah said. "They both are nice enough, but I just can't see eye-to-eye with Pastor Bill and that church of his. Worse yet, Sherriff doesn't go to church at all," Seth said while shaking his head. "You really take this whole church thing seriously, huh?" Elijah replied. Elijah himself was not a religious person. He had left the church long ago; he had left God in that small town in South Carolina where he had grown up. "I take God seriously, I take my faith seriously, and I take God's purpose for my life seriously," Seth said. "The church is just a manifestation of that," he concluded. Elijah could feel the seriousness in Seth's tone; religious Seth seemed to be another person entirely. "I just can't stand the idea that there are people out there that are lost. Even worse, there are people out there that actively oppose God," Seth continued while Elijah remined silent. "I just want to see everyone make it to heaven," Seth concluded on a lighter note. Elijah knew that Seth was active in the church, but he did not realize how deeply religious Seth was. He had assumed that Church was just a small-town requirement, a tradition more than a belief. Though Elijah was not a believer, he admired Seth's passion. "What about you?" Seth said in serious tone; he quickly turned the tables on the conversation. Stammering, Elijah tried to formulate a sensitive reply. He was growing fond of Seth and did not want to ruin the only friendship he currently had in Langford. "I, I, Well, I'm, I'm a, I guess I am…" he barely managed to squeeze out before Seth interjected. "I already know, your Aunt Ruby ask's us to pray for you every Sunday," Seth said. "Deep down in there I know you haven't forgotten about God, I can feel it," he continued. "I'm going to the Church tonight for Wednesday prayer service, go with me?" Seth asked. "Well, I need to…Um, I should," Elijah was again bumbling through an attempt to say the right things while avoiding the subject of church. "What else is there to do? It starts in a couple of hours, let's hang out and then we'll head over." Elijah had developed a soft spot for Seth; he could not say no.

The large white door creaked and groaned as Seth tugged firmly on the door handle to open it. "After you," he said while motioning for Elijah to enter. He cautiously made his way through the doorway; he was unfamiliar with the church itself. The farthest he had ventured was to the parking lot to pick up or drop off ruby, and to the fellowship hall for a community meal. The large room was brightly lit; the lights were almost painfully bright. Directly ahead was a pulpit with a large wooden podium placed dead center. The roughly assembled structure appeared to be homemade; a misshapen cross was carved into the front of it. Large speakers were on both sides of the stage, and musical instruments seemed to be everywhere. There was a drum set, a piano, and a bass on one side of the podium. Several guitars, an organ and a slew of smaller noise makers littered the other side of the pulpit. Rows of pews stretched forward on both sides of Elijah. He then noticed a large cross hanging on the wall behind the stage, on the cross was a crucified and bleeding Jesus Christ. The life-sized savior affixed to the wall and the stereotypical church pews were the only giveaways that Elijah was not at a concert. Elijah would have much rather been at concert in Nashville than heading to a weekday service at The Second Coming Bible Church.

"Well go on," Seth said with a laugh. "No one here bites," he continued. Elijah slowly started making his way down the aisle that separated the two rows of pews. The thick red carpet felt soft through his shoes; looking down he noticed that the carpet was old and worn. It was a thick shag that must have been installed at some point in the 1970's. "Wow, they really have the retro thing down," Elijah thought to himself with a slight chuckle under his breath. He slowed as he was nearing the front of the church, he was not sure where to sit. "Front row on your right is my normal spot," Seth said after noticing that Elijah was lost. Elijah made his way down the row slowly until Seth signaled that he was in the right spot. "Here it is," Seth said as he started to sit down. The old church pew emitted a low groan as Elijah took his seat. The dark stained wooded bench was hard and uncomfortable; it felt cool against Elijah's back. "Aunt Ruby!" Elijah thought to himself in a panic. "Seth, I forgot that I need to bring Aunt Ruby to Church!" he said out loud with concern. "Why? She's walking in now," Seth replied with a smile and a smirk. "How in the…" Elijah softly said under his breath as Seth interjected: "I sent a text message to pastor that we were coming tonight, and that Ruby would need a ride." Elijah's panic slowly turned to relief. "Pastor sent someone over to fetch her," Seth explained. Ruby waived to the two boys as she made her way towards her seat.

A loud and rumbling "boom-boom-boom," pierced the low roar of conversating parishioners. Elijah could feel the thumping low vibration of the noise in his chest. The booming bass was followed by the loud squeal and crackle of an electric guitar coming to life. People scurried to fill any of the vacant instruments Elijah had observed earlier. Soon, a full band had been formed before his very eyes. The sheer volume of the music surprised Elijah; this is not what he had expected it to be. The jingle-jangle of tambourines, the rattle of various noisemakers, and random shouts of praise and worship started to erupt from the crowd. Elijah curiously gazed around the old church; he was enjoying the pure spectacle of it all. The vividly bright overhead lights dimed as he heard commotion from the pulpit; he observed a familiar face preparing to speak.

"Praise God!" Pastor Eldridge shouted from behind the podium. "Praise God!" the congregation echoed back. The pastor shouted even louder, "Praise God!" as he firmly gripped the podium. "Praise God!" the congregation echoed back with a raucous cheer. "Welcome back my flock, let us pray," the pastor said. The music lowered to become barely audible as the Pastor said, "Dear heavenly father let your presence be known. Open our minds to your word and allow us to gain an understanding of your teachings. Bless us lord God, every sheep of this flock. Protect us from the evil that awaits us outside of these doors," Pastor Eldridge prayed out loud. After a few moments of silence, the Pastor uttered, "amen."

The music near instantly turned back to full volume; people were jumping and shouting all over the room. Seth snapped to attention, standing up and raising his hands towards the ceiling. Elijah slowly stood to join him as to not stand out from the crowd. "Praise God, praise God, praise God, praise God," Seth chanted in a loud repeating whisper. Elijah stood there in silence taking in all that was happening around him; this is not what he expected it to be. The long and loud session of praise and worship eventually came to an end. Its official conclusion was noted with a "Be seated children," from Pastor Eldridge. The pastor bellied up to the podium and cleared his throat with a loud cough. "I know it's a prayer service, but y'all know I can't come to church and not preach," Pastor Eldridge said with a laugh. "But before I start preaching, I want to thank God for answering one of our prayers," he continued. "We are joined tonight by Elijah Howard, the nephew of Ruby Morgan." Elijah turned a bright shade of red and quickly looked down at his feet in embarrassment. Blending in had not worked out well for him; Elijah stood out like a sore thumb. Sweat rolled from his brow as the congregation applauded him, Elijah was beyond embarrassed. "Praise be to God for bringing Elijah home to church!" Pastor Eldridge shouted in worship.

"If everyone could turn to 2 Chronicles 15:12-13," Pastor Eldridge said as he thumbed through the already open bible on the podium in front of him. *"And they entered into a covenant to seek the Lord, the God of their fathers, with all their heart and with all their soul, but that whoever would not seek the Lord, the God of Israel, should be put to death, whether young or old, man or woman,"* the pastor read aloud to the church in a fiery tone. "Brothers and sisters, we must not only seek God for ourselves, but we must also demand that those of this world also kneel down before the one true God!" Pastor Eldridge shouted as the church erupted in praise. "The world will bow down before the lord! The world shall bow down before the lord! Jesus Christ is the one true God of this world and all shall kneel before him!" the pastor shouted ferociously. "This world shall see the power of God," he continued. "Repent now before its too late, oh sinners repent in the eyes of this church and the eyes of the one true God!" he shouted while waiving his arms toward the ceiling.

Elijah had only heard stories about churches like this, he had never personally witnessed "fire and brimstone" preaching before. Pastor Eldridge appeared nearly possessed as his body contorted and shook wildly as he screamed his message loudly to the congregation. As he grew louder and louder, the musicians made their way back to their instruments. The music started to slowly grow in volume to match the pastor. Soon there was a thunderous mixture of music and preaching filling the room; the congregation grew just as wild as the pastor. The parishioners screamed and yelled various bits of praise and support to their God. Elijah could distinctly feel the odd mixture of energy filling the church; for the congregation it was a pure release of self. But for him, it was a mixture of fear and curiosity.

As quickly as it started, it seemed to stop. With one small sentence, everything came quickly to order. "Let us pray," Pastor Eldridge said. "Thank you, Lord God, for allowing us another opportunity to glorify your name and fellowship in your house," the pastor prayed aloud. "We are you humble servants and we shall live out your word," he continued. "We shall do all things in your name God! Let us remember the message tonight of 2 Chronicles 15:12-13, and let us do our best to live your words God," the pastor prayed with his eyes shut and arms extend out over the congregation. "Bless us lord god, every sheep of this flock. Protect us from the evil world that awaits us outside of these doors and help us to bring glory to your name while we traverse this foul world God," Pastor Eldridge concluded. Just as the service and began, it ended. The short prayer ended with an "amen," and the night was brought to a close.

"Oh my god!" Elijah shouted as he made his way out on to the front porch of the old Morgan homestead. Ruby had summoned him to come outside with a sharp yell of his name. A large black SUV had just pulled into the driveway; its doors swung open and out poured Elijah's friends from Nashville. "I can't believe you guys actually came," Elijah said cheerfully as he made his way down the steps and towards vehicle. "You know I'm a whore for a good road trip, seeing you is just a bonus," Brit shouted back with a laugh as she dug through the car for her belongings. "Shut up Brit, you're scaring the locals!" Tristan said as he walked towards the back of the SUV to fetch some bags, stopping momentarily to hug Elijah as they crossed paths. "Where is..." Elijah started to say as he was interrupted by Brit. "Hunter?" Brit said finishing his sentence. "He should be here right about..." she said as Hunters black *Mercedes* SUV pulled into the driveway bumping loud and muffled music. "Talk about scaring the locals," Brit said with a chuckle. As the driver's door of the *Mercedes* swung open, the music became instantly louder and then suddenly stopped as Hunter turned-off the car. "Y'all, where have you brought me?" Hunter asked in his deep southern voice while exiting the car. "Welcome to the booming city of Langford," Elijah said while meeting Hunter for a hug. "God, I've missed you guys," Elijah said as he squeezed Hunter in a quick embrace. He then helped them towards the house, laughing and continuing to welcome his little group of friends with a suitcase in each hand.

Ruby awaited the group on the porch; she was rocking in her favorite chair and watching the reunion unfold in the gravel and grass driveway. As they climbed the old creaky steps, Elijah introduced his friends. "This is Brit, Hunter, and Tristan," he said. "They are my friends from Nashville that I've told you about," he continued. Each member of the group took a moment to shake Ruby's hand and introduce themselves; Ruby politely grinned and nodded her head with each introduction. "It is so nice to meet everyone. I have heard so much about each of you," Ruby said as she started to stand from the chair. She moaned out in frustrated pain as she attempted to make it to her feet. Elijah instinctively came to her assistance and helped her to her to stand. "Now come inside, you all must be starving," Ruby instructed as she made her way through the open front door. "I hope you like country cooking," she shouted as she shuffled towards the kitchen.

The kitchen of the old Morgan homestead was soon filled with the smells of Ruby's cooking and the laughter of the reunited friends. It had been a long time since this old house had seen this much life. Until Elijah's arrival, it had been only Ruby for as long anyone cared to remember. "It does my heart good to see so much cheer in this house," Ruby said with a smile. "This reminds me of when I was a little girl, everyone gathered together around the dinner table," she continued. Everyone was stuffing their faces with Ruby's amazing food. There were biscuits, gravy, pork chops, and a pie. Ruby had pulled out all of the stops for the group's arrival. "Mrs. Morgan, you really did not have to do all this. It is amazing!" Brit interjected with a mouth full of biscuit. "It's Aunt Ruby to you dear, and the pleasure is all mine," Ruby replied. "I'm happy to still be able to cook, and even happier to have some folks to cook for," she continued. The remainder of the small group echoed Brit's sentiment, each muttering a "thank you" between bites. "I have made up the guest rooms so y'all take your pick," Ruby instructed. "I'm happy to have you all and you are welcome to stay as long as you'd like," Aunt Ruby said. "I do have a few rules, no drugs, no booze, and no fornication under my roof," she continued. Each of the friends nodded in agreement with her outdated rules and continued to feast upon the delectable meal that Ruby had prepared.

The crickets chirped loudly as lightning bugs filled the warm and humid Tennessee air; the friends were in awe of the sights and sounds of the countryside. They rarely left the sprawling concrete covered topography of downtown Nashville; the alluring and mysterious mixture of farmland and rolling hills was completely new to the group. Their amusement was not lost on Elijah, but he had grown accustomed to the rural beauty of Langford weeks ago. As the group of friends set around a small crackling fire, the chirping of katydids joined the choir of country sounds. "Are they always that loud?" Tristan asked of Elijah referring the noisy katydids. "I think so," Elijah replied. "It's strange, I don't even really notice them anymore," he explained. "Well, they are noisy little shits if you ask me," Brit chimed in. "Time for some more wood," Hunter said will pointing at the shrinking fire. "Come on Elijah, lets get this thing cooking," he continued.

"I think this one will do just fine," Hunter said as he pulled a log from Ruby's woodpile. The katydids and crickets hushed as he crawled from the mound and handed the hefty log to Elijah. Elijah made his way back towards the warm glow of the fire as Hunter continued his search. He tossed the heavy log on the fire, sending bits of glowing embers and ash into the air. He then dusted the bark and dirt from his shirt and set down. After dinner and settling in, the group had decided to celebrate their reunion. Elijah and Hunter had built a small fire in a firepit in the backyard; Aunt Ruby had donated the necessities to make smores. "Tristan, make a smore for Aunt Ruby so I can take it inside to her," Elijah asked. Tristan acknowledged the request with a smile and started the process of constructing the treat for the ailing woman.

"Are you sure you won't join us outside?" Elijah asked while placing the freshly made smore on a small table next to Ruby's recliner. "I am entirely too old, and it is entirely too late for me to do anything other than eat this smore and go to bed!" Aunt Ruby said with a laugh. "Well come on out if you feel like it," Elijah said while patting her on the arm. "We'll probably be out there catching up for most of the evening," he continued. "Don't wait on me," Aunt Ruby replied with a smile. Elijah smiled back and started making his way out of the room. "Let us know if we're too loud," Elijah said turning back momentarily. "Oh hush, go enjoy your friends!" Aunt Ruby said as she turned her attention back to the evening news and the fresh smore that awaited her.

As Elijah made his way through the back door and into the yard, he was hit with a strange yet familiar smell. A pungent, earthy, and sweet smell overcame him. He rushed back to shut the still open back door; he swiftly moved towards the fire to find the culprit. "What the fuck Hunter?" he said in a sharp yet muffled tone. "You can't smoke that shit here!" he continued while pointing at the still smoldering joint in Hunters hand. "Who still smokes joints anyways? What is this, 7th grade?" Brit chimed in with a snorting laugh. "Shut up Brit, you are not helping," Elijah snapped back with frustration. "Ok, ok, ok, everyone be cool and put that shit out Hunter," Tristan said calmly. "Fine! God, calm down." Hunter said while flipping the small burning coal off of the end of the joint. "Three rules, she gave us three rules! Can we please give a dying woman, the dying woman whose house we are staying in, the respect of following her rules?" Elijah said in calm yet stern voice. "What is she smells it? What if she sees it?" he asked. "Things are different here, it's not like Nashville," he concluded. The group quickly put the few moments of drama behind them and settled back in their conversation; a conversation that lasted long into the cool Tennessee night.

"Elijah, wake up! Hey, hey, Elijah," Brit said while shaking Elijah's shoulder. "Ugh, what time is it?" Elijah said replying to her efforts to roust him from bed. "Have you talked to Hunter?" she replied. "Hunter? I talked to him last night, you were there," he answered in a confused daze. "No, since then? I can't find him, he's gone," she explained. Elijah's groggy confusion instantly turned to clarity and concern. "What do you mean he's gone?" Elijah asked, still tying to make sense of what Brit was saying. "I woke up to go to the bathroom and I noticed the door to his room was open. I peaked in to check on him and he was gone," Brit explained. "The bed was made up and his bags were gone. I checked outside, and his car was gone as well," she said. Elijah immediately reached across the bed for his phone that was charging on the nightstand. He tapped on the phone to bring it to life; a message from Hunter greeted him. "He messaged me this morning at 4:13 AM," Elijah said as he unlocked the cell phone to read the text message. "Sorry about last night. I Always seem to ruin the party. Heading back home to cool off and give everyone some space. Talk to you when you get back," Elijah read out loud. "Seems like he got worked up about last night and left," Elijah said. Moments like these were not new for Hunter, he often found himself playing the part of the stereotypical angry alpha-male, hot head, or crying drunk. "Well at least we know he's ok," Brit said. "Normal Hunter, we'll catch up with him back home. Let's just give him some space," she continued.

The murmur of conversations, the clinks of ceramic mugs, and the scrape of utensils against plates filled the diner. "King Kong's Kones, huh?" Brit said with a chuckle and a smirking grin. "Do they realize that the initials..." she started to ask as she was quickly silenced by Elijah. "Shut up Brit! I'm sure they didn't even think about it," he said while motioning to her to keep it down. Elijah had managed to fly under the radar so far and had no intentions of stirring anything up now. His family should be arriving within a few weeks to relieve him of his duties; a few more weeks of keeping his head down and he could finally return home. "Well, the KKK makes a great breakfast!" Tristan said while snorting and trying to contain his laughter. "But how do they manage to keep the hotdog chili off of the white robes?" he continued as his snorting laughter grew louder. Brit was struggling to contain her laugher as she covered her mouth with her hands. Elijah kicked her foot from across the table and elbowed Tristan in the ribs. "Shut up guys! People are staring," he said in a loud and annoyed whisper.

"I'm still not sure how they settled on the name," Tristan stated inquisitively. "Oh god, this again?" Elijah said with a loud sigh as he laid his head back on smooth round back of the vinal booth seat. "No, I'm seriously asking," Tristan said. "They have chili dogs, breakfast, sloppy joes, and I even see a steak dinner on the menu. King Kong's Kones doesn't do the place justice." he explained. "At the very least call it King Kong's Kitchen, KKK!" he said while breaking back into snorting laughter; Brit joining him as Elijah again attempted to silence them. "Time's changed but the name stayed the same," a ragged and shrill voice said while approaching the booth. "This place mostly served ice cream back when there were other places to eat," the old and tired looking waitress said as she filled each of their cups with water. "Times got tough after the farms left, almost everything shut down," she explained. "This old place adapted to meet the need," the waitress continued. "They started cooking and never stopped," she said. "And I've been bitching at them about that damn KKK thing for years. I don't know if it's good or bad that they can't see what's wrong with it!" she concluded laughingly. "Now, can I get you all anything else?" she inquired of the group. "No thank you ma'am, just the check," Elijah politely replied. The waitress nodded and made her way back behind the counter.

"Too bad Hunter couldn't be here for this," Elijah said as the group made their way out of the diner and towards Tristan's large black SUV. "Elijah! Hey

Elijah!" a loud and energetic shout echoed from across the parking lot. Startled, Elijah began scanning the lot to see who was calling him. He near immediately spotted a very familiar rust speckled white Ford pickup truck. "Wait up!" Seth shouted as he came jogging across the parking lot towards the group. "What's up? How have you been? It's been a few days," Seth asked as he caught his breath from the sprint. "I'm good, just been catching up with some friends from Nashville," Elijah replied. "Oh, Hello!" Seth said while waving to the group. "Where are your manners Elijah, are you not going to introduce us?" Brit questioned with a curious grin. "Guys this is Seth," he said. "Seth, this is my best friends Brit and Tristan," he continued. The group exchanged smiles and handshakes as they made introductions.

"Well, it's a pleasure to meet all of y'all," Seth said in his country twang. "It's nice to meet you too Seth," Brit jumped in speaking for the group. "How do you and Elijah know each other?" she curiously asked. "I know him through Ruby, but we officially met at church," he replied. "I just gave him the official Langford town tour the other day, and Eli is planning on showing me Nashville soon!" Seth continued with a smile. "Met at church and taking him to Nashville, huh Eli?" she said while peering at Elijah with a smirking grin. "Elijah never told us he was going to church, and he definitely never told us that there was an official town tour," she said while patting Elijah on the back. Elijah was starting to turn red with embarrassment; this small-town version of himself was not something he was comfortable revealing to his friends. "You guys should come to church with me!" Seth said excitedly. "And if you have time tomorrow, maybe we could all hang out and I could show y'all around?" he continued on to ask. "All we have is time, lets do it!" Brit replied.

"God damnit!" Tristan shouted in annoyance as his large black SUV bounced and scrapped across the large potholes as he entered the parking lot of Lake View Park. "Déjà fucking vu," Elijah muttered replying to Tristan's frustration. "I hit that thing the last time I met Seth here," he said while shaking his head. "Look's like we've beat him here, just park over there so we can see the lake," Elijah continued. Tristan navigated his way into a space with a lake view to appease the requests of the group. Leaving Elijah and Brit behind, he quicky leapt from the car to examine it for damages. "So, this Seth guy?" Brit asked of Elijah curiously.

"What about him?" Elijah replied. "Well, you're going to church with him for starters, you are riding around with him and hanging out, and you're taking him home! What going on?" she asked. "Nothing, I'm just bored, and he was around, so we hung out a bit," he explained. "But you in church? Come on!" she said laughingly. "Either you have a crush on him, he has a crush on you, or both," she continued with a chuckle. They both grew instantly silent as Tristan climbed back into the drivers' seat; Elijah would have to explain himself later. "Just mud, it doesn't look like anything's damaged," he said in an agitated tone. He could sense the awkwardness inside the car, "It's like a funeral in here, what did I miss?" he said with a laugh. "Nothing," they said simultaneously as Seth's old white and rust speckled trucked parked alongside of them.

After some brief re-introductions and catching up, Seth climbed into the front passenger seat of Tristan's car to act as the groups tour guide. Over the next hour, the group near-identically retraced the trail of the original tour Seth had given Elijah. He dutifully pointed out the old bank, along with the new bank they recently built across the street. He advised them of the best gas station in town, shown them The Second

Coming Bible Church, ranted about The Christ Almighty Worship Center, and wrapped everything up at King Kong's Kones for a snack. Brit and Tristan enjoyed the quaintness and charm of the little town of Langford, it was a much-needed break from the urban life they had always known. Elijah was over the change in scenery; his enjoyment came from catching up with old friends and spending time with Seth. "Let's eat!" Seth said excitedly as Tristan pulled into a parking space. Elijah and his group of friends were quickly becoming regulars at King Kongs Kones.

After a brief lunch, one that was filled with chili dogs and packed with further discussion about the history of Langford and her neighboring areas, the group made the journey back to Lake View Park. "Hey man, thank you for showing us around. Let's hang out again soon?" Tristan said while shaking Seth's hand. "Yes!" Brit exclaimed. "You'll have to show us what you and Eli do for fun," she said with a suggestive laugh. The suggestiveness of her comments was lost on Seth. "It was my pleasure, it's great to spend some time with such cool people," Seth said. "Hey, listen, it's Wednesday and there's Church tonight. Would you all like to come?" he added. The three friends glanced at each other in the near-telepathic way that close friends do, they concluded that they had no desire to go to church. "Raincheck?" Brit responded. "We're pretty tired and plus we hoped to hog Elijah to ourselves for a bit," Tristan chimed in. "It's been so long since we've hung out, we'd like to just spend some time together," he concluded. "Oh, I get it," Seth replied in disappointment. "Maybe we can come for Sunday service?" Elijah replied in an effort to cheer up Seth. "What do you say guys?" he asked prompting his friends to commit. "Yeah, Sunday could work," Brit mumbled in agreement. "That's great news!" Seth said excitedly. "I've got to run, but I'll see you then!" he continued as he opened the door to his old white pickup. "See y'all!" Seth shouted as he rolled down the old crank-style window and started his vehicle. The truck then roared and squeaked its way off into the distance.

"Well, I guess we are church-goers now," Tristan said with a laugh. "We have a few days before we have to give up our sinful ways," Brit said as she pulled a bottle of *Jägermeister* from under the back seat of the SUV. "Of all the things you could bring, you bring that nasty shit," Tristan said. "Hey, it's Elijah's favorite and this is his party," she replied while smiling at Elijah.

"Come on guys, lets get this party started!" she exclaimed as she started dancing her way from the car and towards the lake. Tristan and Elijah locked eyes and smiled at Brits excitement; the pair ran towards the lake to catch up with her. The two hopped and jumped from leg-to-leg, wrestling to remove their clothes and shoes before proceeding down to the water's edge. The red clay felt cold and squishy between Elijah's toes, this was a far cry from the sandy beach he expected it to be. Brit was mid-drink by the time Elijah and Tristan caught up to her. "Your turn!" she said with laugh as she handed the bottle to Elijah. He turned it up and took two full gulps before passing it to Tristan. "Race you to the water!" Elijah said as he took off running. Brit followed quickly behind him in pursuit. "Hey, wait up!" Tristan shouted as he swiftly took a drink, threw the bottle down, and chased after his two friends.

"Nope! Nope! Nope!" Elijah shouted as he crashed into the murky green water. It was too late for Brit to heed his warnings; she crashed into the freezing water right behind him. "God damnit that's cold!" she screamed as she ran back towards the slippery red clay bank. Tristan greeted them at the edge of the water laughing, "Serves you right!" he said as he continued to chuckle at their blunder. They quickly passed him up and raced back towards the car to fetch a towel. Being the "mother" to the group, Brit was ever prepared for anything. After digging momentarily through her oversized bag, she pulled out a faded beach towel. She swiftly patted herself dry and then handed the towel to Elijah. "Hey guys, come take a look at this," Tristan shouted up from the shoreline. Elijah tossed the towel back in the car and they made their way back down to the water.

"Check it out, there's a trail," Tristan said while pointing down the rocky clay shoreline. The small carved out beach area was surrounded by tall trees and thick undergrowth. The barren swimming area was an anomaly compared to the rest of the visible shoreline. In the middle of the thick line of trees that walled off the beach was a small break in the dense vegetation; there was a narrow and well-worn trail. "Who's up for a hike?" Tristan asked. Brit and Elijah gazed at each other still shivering from their dip in the chilly lake. "Right now?" Elijah asked. "I'm freezing!" he added as Brit shook her head in agreement. "Oh, toughen up you two!" Tristan replied callously. "Fine, let's warm up in the car and work on this bottle. Then can we explore the trail?" he asked persuasively. "Fine, but I need to catch a good buzz before I'll be willing to go galivanting in the woods," Brit replied. "Ok, fine!" Elijah replied.

The heated leathers seats and warm cab of the SUV made quick work of the freezing friends; the *Jägermeister* didn't hurt either. "Why do you want to run off into the woods anyways? Who knows where that trail even goes?" Elijah said still questioning Tristan's proposal. "Exactly!" Tristan said with excitement. "Now that I know that it exists, I have to find out where it goes! That's half of the excitement," Tristan replied. "What's the other half of the excitement?" Brit chimed in with a strong dose of sarcasm. "The chance that I might see a deer or a bear, that's the other half!" Tristan exclaimed laughingly. The car erupted in giggles at the absurdity of the Tristan's answer. "You had me at bear, I'm in!" Elijah replied. "Ok, I think we are intoxicated enough to start this adventure. Let's go!" Brit said as she opened her door and made her way from the car. "Bring the booze!" she shouted back to Tristan and Elijah.

The leaves and small bits of branches and acorns crunched under their feet; they cautiously made their way beyond the trailhead and into the dense forest. The bright sun-filled sky was quickly shut out by the overgrowth. The group now found themselves in the dimly lit woods; a sea of green and brown engulfed them. While cautiously avoiding the long arms of briars that laid across the path, the friends forged forward. "Does everything in this godforsaken place have fucking thorns on it?" Brit asked in frustration as she plucked small slivers of briars from her sweatshirt. The daylight diminished with each step farther into the forest, the vegetation grew thicker and the trail grew narrower. The friends marched forward, determined to make the most out of their day.

"Well, I don't think we are charting any new territory," Tristan said to the group as he pointed to a small, ragged piece of red and black fabric hanging from the briar patch in front of him. "Look guys, there's a wide spot up ahead!" Brit shouted. The group punched through the last patch of briars and trees ahead of them swiftly; a small circular clearing greeted them on the other side. From the small circular field jetted three other trails, all going in different directions. In the middle of the grassy clearing were several logs with a small stone fire pit in the center. "It looks like a campsite," Elijah said as he walked around the clearing observing what they had discovered. He plopped down on one of the logs and Brit and Tristan joined him. As quickly as she had taken a seat, Brit leapt from the log and exclaimed, "Look! There's the water! I'm going to check it out," dashing down the trail in front of them. "Stay close!" Tristan shouted as she disappeared back into the dense woods.

"You have to admit that this is nice," Elijah said to Tristan as the pair sat observing their serene surroundings. They were encapsulated in the dense, green wilderness. They were encompassed by silence; only the knock of a woodpecker or the sounds of playful squirrels encroached on the noiseless wall of trees that surrounded them. "I've missed you," Tristan replied. "Being apart has really made me come to terms with some things," he continued. Elijah gazed back at him waiting to see what he would say next. Back when Elijah had first moved to Nashville, and Brit had introduced Tristan to him, they immediately hit it off. This had all been part of Brit's master plan; Brit knew Elijah long before Elijah knew himself. Ever the matchmaker, Brit introduced the two with hopes that they would blossom into a couple. Neither were "out" to themselves at the time, much less the group, but Brit had a near sixth sense about these sorts of things. Elijah and Tristan indeed hit off, but the pressures of work, life, self-discovery, and being closeted quickly turned the fiery and lustful relationship sour. "I can't explain how much I miss you Elijah, how much I miss us," Tristan continued. The two had recently shared a brief fling before again pausing things to assess the situation. But Elijah had strong feelings for Tristan, feelings he had never experienced before or since meeting him. Elijah's eyes filled with tears; he had longed to try things again with Tristan for some time now. "I miss you," Elijah replied as he laid his head on Tristan's shoulder. The pair sat in silence for a few brief moments just enjoying the simplicity of the moment.

The surrounding silence was broken by the sounds of breaking branches, loud crunches of leaves, and panicked shouting. The noise grew louder and louder; Elijah and Tristan jumped from the log preparing for whatever might emerge from the forest. A disheveled and shaken Brit stepped from the tree line and into the clearing. Now realizing that it was Brit,

Elijah and Tristan ran to meet her. "Brit, what's wrong?" Elijah shouted in concern. "What happened Brit?" Tristan said. She did not immediately reply to their questions, she just stood there with tears rolling from her eyes and clinching something in her hands. She was pale, shaken, and frightened. Something had happened on her journey to the lakes shore. Elijah started looking her over, he could find no apparent signs that she had been hurt. "What going on? You look like you have seen a ghost," he said with a chuckle as he attempted to break the tension of the conversation. She snapped to attention and glanced at him, her eyes red and swollen from her tears. She silently extended her arms to reveal what she was clinging to.

As her hands opened, she revealed a mud-covered cell phone with a shattered screen. Elijah and Tristan stared at each other with confusion. "Oh, I'm sorry Brit," Tristan said empathetically. "It's ok Brit, we can run over to Lola and get you a new phone," Elijah added. "It's just a broken phone, its nothing to cry over," He continued as he wrapped his arms around her. Without saying a word, Brit reached into her back pocket and pulled out her phone. The boy's confusion grew deeper as they waited for an explanation. "That's not my phone and I didn't break it," Brit finally said. "I found it half-buried in the mud down by the shore," she added. "It still works she said," as she pressed a button on the side of the phone. The device brightly lit up revealing a barely visible picture on the lock screen of the phone. I was a group picture of Tristan, Brit, Elijah, and Hunter. "What the fuck," Tristan shouted. "Whose phone is that? What kind of creep has a picture of us on their phone out here?" He said as he grew angrier and louder. Brit started tapping on her phone, the other phone sprang to life vibrating in her other hand. She turned her phone to Tristan and Elijah to reveal the truth; she was calling Hunter.

IV

"I didn't think they actually did this in real life," Tristan said attempting to break the silence. The group of friends were standing in the parking lot of Lake View Park wrapped in thick wool blankets and surrounded by firetrucks and police cars. Upon discovering Hunter's phone, they had run from the woods and called 9-1-1. The first responders were combing the woods looking for Hunter. "Howdy y'all, I'm Deputy Randy Ward," a rough and mean looking man said as he approached the group. Elijah recognized him from the church; the man just had this unforgettable look about him. Randy Ward had a look that invoked fear in Elijah. Deputy Ward was a wolf. "So, let me give you an update," Deputy Ward continued. "We have found no evidence of foul play, it seems he might have simply lost his phone or tossed it out," Randy continued. "What the hell? Brit shouted. "There is no way, Hunter would..." she continued as the deputy cut her off. "Ma'am don't raise your voice to me," Deputy Ward said sternly. "All signs point to him doing exactly what he told Elijah he was doing, cooling off," Deputy Ward continued. "He texted Elijah that he needed some space and he left town, I'm sure that he's back in Nashville right now enjoying some solitude," Deputy Ward concluded. "There's the sheriff, I better fill him in," the deputy said as he pointed to a shiny new black *Impala* that entered the parking lot. Deputy Ward left the group to speak with his superior. "Somethings wrong," Brit said in a worried tone, "I can just feel it, something is wrong," she repeated.

A day came and went; the friends had yet to contact Hunter. They each called friends in Nashville and spent their day in Langford looking for Hunter to no avail. The only update that Deputy Ward provided was that there was no evidence to indicate any crime or wrongdoing. The deputy was certain that Hunter had simply "went off the grid" for a while and refused to file a missing person's report. "Maybe he did just take some time away," Elijah said to Brit and Tristan as they grabbed some lunch at King Kong's Kones. "I just cannot believe that" Brit replied. Tristan shrugged his shoulder admitting the possibility that Hunter could have in fact run away for some personal time. "All I'm saying is that this is not out of the realm of possibility for Hunter," Elijah continued. "Let's just give him a few days, and if we do not hear anything we can go to the Sheriff? Better yet, we can drive to Nashville for a day to check on him?" Elijah asked. "Ok, fine!" Brit replied. "But if that doesn't work or we can't find him, we are going to the state police," she concluded.

"Elijah! Brit! Tristan!" a deep southern voice shouted from across the restaurant. It was Seth, he had been sitting with a group of parishioners from the church. He ran across to greet the group of friends. "How are y'all doing? Did you find your friend yet?" he asked inquisitively. "No, not yet" Elijah replied. "Well, I'm sure it's just like Deputy Ward said, He's probably just run off to find himself or something," Seth said. "Wait, how do you know what the Deputy said? Brit replied somewhat confused. "Eh, it's a small town and going to church with the deputy doesn't hurt," Seth said with a little chuckle. "It's not all gossip," He continued as he shifted to a more serious tone. "The church has been praying for him," he said. The group of friends stared blankly at one another as silence fell over the table. Elijah finally looked up to acknowledge Seth; he was always taken back by how tall Seth was. Seth loomed over the booth wearing a well-worn baseball cap and a bright red and black flannel shirt. "Thank you, Seth, we really do appreciate that," Elijah said sincerely. "Will you please keep an eye-out? You know this place better than anyone," he continued. Seth acknowledged his request with a nod and a smile before turning to make his way back towards his table. Elijah couldn't help but stare; he definitely had some amount desire for Seth. As he stared at Seth walking away, he noticed a small tear in the back of his shirt. The small, frayed hole stood out to Elijah because Seth was so normally well kempt. A sharp, stabbing pain jolted Elijah back to reality. The source of the pain made itself known; it was a swift kick in the shin under the table from Tristan. "Hey! I'm over here!" Tristan said with an obvious and deserved tone of jealousy. Brit stared harshly at Elijah; their best friend ESP was working well. He knew exactly what she was thinking – *"This is not part of the plan! You and Tristan are perfect together. Fix this dumbass!"* Elijah took a moment to formulate his thoughts before responding. "I'm sorry, its really not what you think," he said. "I've been lonely here and I have enjoyed the attention from Seth, but that would never happen," he continued. "I know what I want and it's not Seth; he's just been a friendly face," he said firmly as he locked eyes with Tristan. The pair stared longingly into each other's eyes for a few quiet moments before being interrupted by Brit. "Plus, he's way too straight, and he's way too churchy to ever not be!" Brit exclaimed in a snorting cackle. The table burst into laughter; her snappy comeback was a momentary escape from the potential gravity of the situation. No one had heard from or seen hunter in days, their friends in Nashville hadn't crossed paths with him since he had departed for Langford, and with the discovery of his phone, good news did not seem to be in sight. But Brit always had a knack for lightening the mood. This brief departure from reality was exactly what the friends needed, but Langford is far to small of a place to hide from reality for very long.

The weekend was soon upon them, and Hunters whereabout were still unknown. Elijah had managed to keep his cool, but he too was growing bothered by the oddness of the situation. Hunter was known to go "M-I-A," but never for this long. Making good on his promise, the group drove across the tiny town in search of the Sheriffs department. After a few laps around Langford, Elijah finally searched for its location on his phone, only to discover that it was in Lola, Tennessee. "Well y'all, I guess we get to explore Lola," he said to his friends as his phone started emitting audible directions. The tires of Tristan's SUV made a loud squeal as he pulled a U-turn to follow the phones directions. This was a path that Elijah recognized, only now, they were going away from Langford rather than towards it. This was the route that Seth had brought him on his first "Grand Tour" of Langford. The small two-lane road was soon engulfed with dark-green trees and foliage; the bright warm sun soon disappeared behind the overgrown canopy of trees. The group weaved their way through the dense forest highway; Tristan's SUV made quick work of the winding road. Soon, the forest gave way to wide open pastureland. Cows and the occasional barn dotted the surrounding fields. A sign soon emerged – *15 miles to Lola.*

Lola felt worlds apart from Langford; it felt like a proper town. Even though the nature of their trip was unpleasant, the group could not contain their giddiness and excitement for the opportunity to enjoy some of the "creature comforts" only Lola could provide in this part of Tennessee. They looked in awe as they passed several well-established restaurants. "I want sushi!" Tristan exclaimed. "No, steak!" Brit shouted from the backseat. All eyes were now on Elijah; he stared out of the passenger side window while pretending to ignore their eager glances. "Mmmm, shrimp tempura roll," he muttered casually. "Fuck you!" Brit shouted. "This is completely unfair; you have to agree with him!" she continued. "Don't hate on our love! Sushi it is!" Tristan shouted back at her victoriously. His comments hit Elijah like a brick, "Our love," he thought to himself. The two had never had the talk about the "L" word, but now he was completely enamored by the thought of it. For the first time in his life Elijah knew for a fact that he was in love – Elijah was in love with Tristan. "Fine! But then you're taking my ass to a mall. Mama needs some new clothes," Brit chimed in. Her comment near instantly snapping Elijah from his newly discovered love-drunk stupor. Reality then punched Elijah in the mouth, the real reason behind their journey found its way into the vacuum created by the departure of his thoughts about being in love with Tristan. "But first we need to talk to the Sheriff" he quietly and calmly stated. Silence overcame the car; behind the vail of silence was the shared fear about the mystery of Hunter's disappearance.

"Take a seat, the Sheriff will be with you shortly." A small portly red-faced man in a dark-brown police uniform said from behind a thick-glass window with a kind smile. The man reminded Elijah of his boss, Bill Porter. His red face and jovial tone made the resemblance uncanny. Seeing Mr. Porters doppelganger placed Elijah at ease. This coincidence calmed Elijah's nerves, even if just for a moment. The small waiting area smelled of stale coffee and old cigarettes; cigarettes that had probably been smoked in the room long before any of the friends were even born. A small old television mounted in the corner of the room quietly played reruns of daytime courtroom dramas, while an occasional ringing phone or radio squawk would come from behind the glassed-off offices. "Hey kids, the Sherriff will see you now," the deputies muffled voice called from behind the glass. A sharp "Bzzzzz" was followed by a loud "click" as the group approached the large gray metal door adjacent to the window. "Down the hall and to the right, you can't miss it," the deputy said as they passed by the front desk. The smell of coffee distilling to sludge was now overpowering, it only grew stronger the farther they proceeded into the police station. After a short moment of wandering, they took a sharp right and were greeted by a large oak door. "Sherriff," it read in black stenciled letters. "Well, I think we're in the right place," Brit said sarcastically. "If you're looking for the sheriff you would be correct, if you've broken the law, I would say that you are in the exact wrong place," a deep voice said from behind the door as it opened. "Elijah!" Sherriff Morales said with surprise, remembering Elijah from the restaurant. "I didn't know it was you waiting out there, hell if I did, I wouldn't have made you wait so long," the sheriff said with a laugh. "I heard that there were people from Langford here, I guessed it was more folks from that damn Second Coming Church here to complain about the noise from Bill's church," he explained. "I move all the way out here from Arizona only to be stuck in the middle of some bull shit church turf war, who would have thought?" he said. Sheriff Morales motioned the group into his office. "How's your Aunt? I keep on the deputies to stop by and check on her when they are over her way," the sheriff asked with sincere concern. "She's hanging in there," Elijah replied. "Well, that's good to hear. Let's get down to business, what's going on?" Sheriff Morales inquired.

"Were here to talk about Hunter," Brit said before Elijah could get in another word. The sheriff walked behind the group and shut the door before setting down at his desk.

The friends laid out their list of concerns while the sheriff dutifully listened; Brit grew more and more argumentative as the conversation continued. Sheriff Morales's expression grew more puzzled the more that he heard. Finally, he chimed in, "why didn't you share all of this when he went missing?" he asked inquisitively. "What the hell? We did!" Brit shouted back at him. Sheriff Jackson Morales was always cool, calm, and collected. He had the same look Elijah recognized in some of the men at Ruby's church; the "I've seen things" look. But the sheriff was different, he was kind and welcoming. The sheriff had seen firsthand the evils of humanity and wanted nothing more than to be part of offsetting all the awful things he had encountered in his life. Sheriff Jackson Morales was a wolf in his own right, but a wolf on the right side of the law. "I get that you are upset, but I need to understand what's going on here," Sheriff Morales calmly replied to Brit. After a few moments of rummaging around in his desk, he pulled out a manila folder. Inside was a few loose pieces of paper; a police report. The sheriff scanned quickly over the folders contents in silence before looking back up at the group of concerned friends sitting before him. He closed his eyes and shook his head; he then placed the folder back in his desk. "What in the god damn hell," he muttered under his breath.

"Tell me about this Hunter?" the Sherriff asked. Brits emotions were now on full display; her protectiveness of her little band of misfits could not be hidden. "Jesus God Damn Christ!" she exclaimed near involuntary. "What do you need to know? He's our friend, he lives in Nashville, he's a Gemini, he hates tequila, loves Thai food, is 34 years-old, and is a good guy that can be a bit of a cunt sometimes," Brit continued sarcastically. "Something like that Sherriff? Oh, and he's been missing for fucking days!" she concluded while crossing her arms and slumping back in her chair. Sheriff Jackson Morales silently listened to her frustrated comments; he swiftly jotted notes on a bright-yellow legal pad laying on his desk. After a few tense moments of the sheriff staring at what he had written down, the "tap-tap-tap" of his ink pen against the pad broke the quietness. "So, since that night at

Ruby's place you haven't seen or heard from him at all?" the sheriff asked as he continued trying to wrap his mind around what had actually happened. The group in unison uttered "no." Elijah grabbed Brits leg to calm her uncontrolled foot tapping; this was a "tick" that manifested in both of them when their nerves were on edge. "So, he shows up in Langford with y'all, he drives his own car here, something happens in the early morning hours while staying at Ruby's, and now nothing?" the sheriff recounted with the group in an effort to get the facts straight. "What about his phone sheriff?" Tristan asked of the stoic lawman. "His phone?" sheriff asked with an oblivious look pouring over his face.

"You're telling me that you found his phone?" Sheriff Morales asked with concern. "Yeah, Brit found it when we were hanging out at Lake View." Elijah calmly stated. "Deputy Ward took it after he wrote down our information for the report." Tristan chimed in. "You were there sheriff, we saw you pull in while we were talking to Deputy Ward." Elijah said. The group now seemed as confused as Sheriff Jackson Morales himself. "Somethings not right here, somethings not right here, what the fuck is going on, this doesn't fit together," the sheriff whispered under his breath while "tap-tap-tapping" his pen harder against the bight-yellow legal pad. "Well, you've got my attention." Said the sheriff. "I don't know what to make of all this yet, but things don't add up." He then said. The group listened attentively, waiting patiently to hear what the sheriff would say next. Their concern for Hunter had only grown from their with chat with the sheriff; Elijah had hoped that this meeting would have the opposite effect. "I don't know what's going on, but before I say anything else, this stays between us four for the time being, ok?" the sheriff stated in a firm and questioning tone. Elijah, Tristan, and Brit glanced at one another before turning and nodding in agreement with the sheriffs request for secrecy.

"The official report makes no mention of most of what you've just told me." Sheriff Morales informed the three concerned friends; they mumbled to each other in confusion as they tried to make sense of what they were hearing. The sheriff, reading aloud from the report:

"While hiking the trails at Lake View park, the kids became concerned about the whereabouts of a missing

friend. Something led them to believe that the possible missing person was at Lake View, so they called to report the person in question as missing. The group stated that the friend had been missing for a few days and had informed them via text message that he was returning to the Nashville area after a brief argument on the night the person in question departed. The group also stated that this is typical behavior for the person in question. My preliminary investigation indicates no foul play and I see no reason to pursue this matter further. I detected a faint smell of alcohol upon initial questioning of the three and believe that intoxication played a role in the sudden desire to file a report – this appears to be a form of retaliation against the person in question for their part in the argument / leaving the trip before it had met its conclusion."

The sheriff closed the folder and tossed it back on his desk. He firmly pushed against the rolled edge of the dark mahogany desk with his hands, leaning back in his chair. "So, you're telling me this is all bull shit?" the sheriff inquired. "Mostly!" Brit snapped back angrily. Elijah again grabbed Britts knee to stop her feverish leg shaking, he then glanced at Tristan to signal him to offer an explanation to the sheriff. Elijah simply did not have it in him to go over the events yet again; his cool and calm demeanor had only been a disguise for how concerned he truly was for Hunter. Elijah had secretly maintained a constant knot in his stomach since the morning Brit had jostled him awake to tell him that Hunter was gone. In an effort to not cause further panic for his friends, he maintained an optimistic tone. But something did not set well with him about the message from Hunter, it just seemed "off." Despite his best efforts, Tristan could see through Elijah's charade. Even with their "on again, off again" relationship, Tristan and Elijah shared a connection that seemed predetermined. They were what some would describe as soulmates, or as "meant to be." Through this near spiritual connection, Tristan clearly understood what Elijah was asking of him with his swift glance.

Tristan snapped into action, he started at the very beginning of their journey to Langford and explained every detail in minutia. He explained their arrival, their early dinner with Ruby, and how the friends spent their first evening catching up around the fire. He openly disclosed that Hunter was a bit of a "pothead," and that him smoking a joint is what led to the disagreement. He explained that they would never "retaliate" against

Hunter, that they were best friends, and that they had indeed shared a bottle of *Jägermeister* at the lake but were nowhere near intoxicated. The sheriff nodded in understanding and carefully took notes as he listened to Tristan explain that the "fight," wasn't really a fight and that they had quickly patched things up and resumed their normal banter. While Tristan explained the text message that Elijah had received, Elijah handed his phone to the sheriff for examination. He continued on to explain that Tristan would sometimes lose his temper, but that he had never ditched them like this in the past. He then talked about what had happened at Lake View, he explained that Brit had found the phone, and how they confirmed that it was Hunters. Tristan detailed the groups interaction with Deputy Randy Ward, their attempts to locate Hunter after filling the report with the deputy, and their plan to go to Nashville for a day of searching. Before Sheriff Morales could respond, Elijah commented "He's an ass hole sheriff, but he's our ass hole. Under all of that he's a really good guy and this is not like him. He wouldn't leave us to worry like this." Brit was now the one grabbing Elijah's knee to calm him. Elijah could no longer hide his concern behind his stoic demeanor. "We're going to find out what's going on here." The sheriff said in a mixture of frustration and anger. "Go to Nashville and let me know if you find anything." The sheriff continued. He wrote down a series of numbers on a small scrap of paper and slid it across the desk, along with Elijah's phone, to the friends. "This is my personal cell, call me when you're back?" he asked. "Don't tell anyone why you're going and don't let anyone know that I'm involved. This is between us for the time being." He then said. "I'm going to do some digging on my end and then we can regroup and figure out what comes next." He concluded. After a few more minutes of conversation the meeting was over, the sheriff stood and shook each of their hands. He made his way from behind the large desk and around to open the door. Sheriff Morales then hugged Brit and said, "we're going to figure this out, I promise you that." The sheriff had a big heart and would occasionally wear it on his sleeve. He was a wolf, but more importantly, he was a good man. If you were in trouble, Jackson Morales is exactly who you'd want in your corner.

"Has it always been this bright?" Brit asked from the backseat of Tristan's large black SUV. Elijah and Tristan laughed at her question; the couple's hands still locked together in a loving embrace from the long journey from Langford. Elijah turned from the passenger's seat to face Brit, his knees on the slippery leather seat cushion. "You've been in God's country for a week and you've already forgotten Nashville?" Elijah asked of her laughingly. "Elijah! Seatbelt!" Tristan shouted with a swift smack on his bottom. Elijah spun back around in his seat and buckled up. "You can't really understand how big this place is until you've been in such a tiny town I guess." Tristan said in a more serious response to Brit's question. "So, this is what it was like the first time you came here from South Carolina Elijah?" Brit asked of her best friend. "Yeah, pretty much. Just imagine living in Lanford for 25 years and then coming here, then you'll have an idea of what it was like." He said with a chuckle. "Fuck that!" Brit shouted in response. "You still have to take me." Tristan inserted while again grabbing Elijah's hand. Elijah looked at him puzzled, "Take you where?" he asked. "To South Carolina" Tristan explained. "I want to see where you grew up, meet some of your childhood friends, and I need to meet your mom at some point." Tristan continued. Elijah was flooded with emotions at the thought of Tristan meeting his mother. He was excited by the idea, but because neither were completely "out," he was also terrified. The idea of coming out to his family always scared Elijah; the religious nature of his family made it seem next to impossible. But Elijah had now come to terms with the fact that he was in love with Tristan. That love meant coming out sooner than later if he wanted the relationship to last. "Guys, it's good to be back for a few minutes." Tristan said. Despite being glad to see their home, the friends had a mission before them. The excitement of the couple's potential future, and the joy of being back home was curbed by a singular and looming question: Where is Hunter?

"Well, his cars not here." Elijah said as they pulled into Hunters driveway. The group made their way to his front door and knocked several loud knocks before Tristan shouted, "Hey Hunter, are you there buddy?" The friends waited patiently for several long minutes, but there was no response. Brit peered through the windows trying to discern if he was home, but all was quiet. Elijah checked Hunters mailbox only to discover that no one had retrieved the mail in at least a few days. It didn't appear that hunter was home or that he had returned since his trip to Langford. "Where to next, guys?" Tristan asked. "We've already checked at his office and they haven't seen or heard from him. I guess we can stop by or normal coffee shop and maybe check at a few of the bars we hang out at?" Elijah asked. After hours of scoping their usual haunts and checking with friends, their efforts devolved into driving around aimlessly in search of Hunter – each of them secretly hoping that they would spot him standing on a corner like a lost puppy waiting to be found. As the day swiftly turned to night, they made their way to Elijah's loft in downtown. With their heads hung low in defeat and their bodies exhausted from the search, they could do more today.

"Elijah, are you awake?" Tristan said while gently nudging Elijah's shoulder to wake him. "Ugh, what time is it?" Elijah asked. "It's a little after midnight. You fell asleep on the couch, now come on, let's get you to bed." Tristan said as he helped Elijah from the couch. Elijah began pulling off his clothes as the two made their way towards his bedroom, leaving a trail of jeans and a shirt behind him. Elijah's home, like his new Lexus, was a symbol of the success he had discovered in Nashville. His hard work had allowed him to live a life that he could only dream of while growing up in South Carolina. But Elijah's large and swank downtown loft always left him feeling empty.

He had moved into it from his seedy first apartment, the complex where he had first met Brit, and during his first relationship with Tristan. Secretly, he moved in hoping that their relationship would blossom and that the two would soon live together. But not long after he was settled the couple broke things off; neither were ready to break the silence on their sexual orientations to the world. Neither realized that what they had was special at the time; they went their sperate ways while vowing to "always remain best friends." They kept good on that promise; a promise that ultimately led them to now discovering their love for each other.

Elijah removed his last scraps of clothes in preparation for sleep, standing now naked next to his plush bed and extending his arms towards the ceiling in a long stretch. Tristan was awestruck by his masculine beauty; he had continued to long for Elijah since the couples last breakup. Even though they were again fanning the flames of their love, the two had not been intimately together since they last parted romantic ways. Tristan followed suit and stripped down to his underwear. He approached Elijah from behind, wrapping his arms around him and nuzzling his face into Elijah's neck. In his sleepiness, Elijah was caught off guard, but soon welcomed the embrace by pushing his body firmly back against Tristan's suggestively. Their passionate embrace soon turned to foreplay, and foreplay turned to intercourse. Elijah emitted a loud muffled moan as Tristan pushed into him; Tristan had placed his hand over Elijah's mouth in hopes of not waking Brit with their antics. In this moment, they both knew that they were meant for one another. "I love you," Tristan whispered into Elijah's ear. "I love you and I always have," he continued as he again slowly thrust into Elijah. The couple fell asleep intertwined in each other's bodies, both comforted by the re-establishment of their "on again, off again" relationship. Their comfort came from the knowing that this time, it was different.

As Elijah slept, he dreamed vivid visions of his future with Tristan. It was like he was truly peering into the future and observing what was to come next. He briefly woke from his slumber and whispered, "I love you, too." to Tristan before dozing back off. The visions of his carefree future did not return to visit him, they were instead replaced with nightmares of Hunter and Langford. In his dream state, he was screaming and yelling Hunter's name, he was searching endlessly for him in a dark void. He then found himself wandering through the woods at Lake View Park, the same woods he and his friends had explored just days before their trip to Nashville. As he walked aimlessly through the dense forest, he found Ruby standing in the field where he and Tristan had sat together on a log; the clearing near where Brit had found Hunter's phone. Ruby was standing in the center of the clearing and pointing towards the lake. "Ruby! Aunt Ruby! What is it?" Elijah called out in his dream. Aunt Ruby just stared blankly at him and smiled. "What is it?!" he shouted loudly at the old woman. She turned and walked from the clearing towards the water's edge, she did not stop as Elijah chased after her calling her name. She walked down the rocky bank and into the water, never stopping. She then slowly disappeared into the dark black water of the lake. Elijah stood on the bank in shock from what he had just witnessed, but before he could even respond he saw the top of her head emerging from the water. She slowly reappeared from the murky depths of the lake; she was carrying the bloated and lifeless body of Hunter. She met him on the rocky beach and dropped the decomposing body at his feet. Fluid from the bloated corpse splattered across Elijah's body, the smell of death flooded his nostrils. "What the fuck is this

Ruby?" he shouted at the old woman. Finally breaking her silence, she screamed out, "whoever would not seek the Lord, the God of Israel, should be put to death, whether young or old, man or woman!"

"Elijah, wake up!" Tristan shouted while shaking him firmly. Tristan's touch pulled him quickly from the hellacious dreamscape in which he was emerged. "Fuck!" Elijah said with a sigh as he set up in his bed. "Woah, what was that? You kept screaming at Ruby in your sleep." Tristan said. "Just a shitty nightmare" Elijah replied while giving Tristan a swift kiss on the lips. The bedroom door burst open and Brit ran in, bellyflopping on the bed between Tristan and Elijah. "What's up bitches? How did you sleep?" she said. "Before you respond to that, let me tell you that I slept like shit." She stated sarcastically. "Awwww, uhhhh, I love you, mmmm, daddy harder, ooOOOOoo, deeper, faster, is all I could hear Elijah!" she said impersonating Elijah's noises from the night before. Elijah slid under the blankets in embarrassment, his red face was in stark contrast to the white blankets on his bed. Brit quickly pulled the covers from him and continued to parody the couple's long night of sex, pretending to be Tristan, and climbing on top of Elijah all the while mimicking Tristan's deep voice. "Get off of me!" Elijah screamed in embarrassment. "Get off in you, you mean?" Brit shouted back while continuing to mimic Tristan's voice. "Give me that ass daddy!" Brit blurted out in a deep voice. Elijah burst out into laughter; he could no longer contain himself. Brit always seemed to know when and how to make Elijah laugh. After the vicious and ominous nightmare he just experienced, Brits jokes were a welcome reprieve. After a few more friendly jabs and some chit chat, Brit grabbed the two men around their necks in a hug. "Awww my babies are all grown up," she said with a slight chuckle. "But really, I love you guys." She continued while squeezing their necks harder. "I also love that you two love each other." She mentioned sincerely.

"There are so many god damn cows. Why the fuck are there so many cows?" Brit blurted out from the backseat as she surveyed the nothingness outside of the car. "For all of those steaks you love," Elijah responded sarcastically to her question. Brit Platts was not your normal "girly girl." She was a little rough around the edges, she liked whisky over wine, preferred steak to salad, knew how to shoot a gun, could and would kick your ass if you needed it, and was fiercely loyal to those that she loved. "Yay, we're halfway back to the middle of nowhere," Brit then muttered as they passed a large green milage sign on the side of the road. The group had come up short in Nashville and after a quick restock of clothes and other necessities, they were heading back to Langford. There had been no trace of Hunter; they each were hopeful that "no news was good news." "We need to call Sheriff Morales," Elijah said. "Hopefully, he's had better luck than we have," he continued. After many miles of desolation, Elijah's cell phone finally found service. His phone, still connected to Tristan's car from the music they were listening to, clacked loudly as he typed the sheriff's number into his phone from a small scrap of paper he retrieved from his pocket. The call trilled loudly over the car's speakers, and after several rings a familiar voice picked up on the other side. "Sheriff Jackson Morales," the rough deep voice said. "Hey sheriff, it's Elijah, Tristan, and Brit. We're on our way back to Langford and wanted to see if you had heard anything." Elijah responded. The sheriff paused for a few moments and then said, "Hey folks, listen, come by my office as soon as you get into town. Just come straight to the Sheriffs Office if you can." "What's going on? Did you find out anything?" Brit chimed in before Elijah could respond. "Look, I think its better if we talk in person. Just come to my office." The sheriff reiterated. "How was Nashville? Did you hear anything?" the sheriff said in attempts to steer the conversation away from the friend's persistent barrage of questions. "Nothing, no one has seen him. His house looked untouched. It looks like he hasn't been home since he left for Lanford." Elijah explained. "Well, just take your time and get here safe." Said Sheriff Morales. In a brief pause in the conversation, the group could hear people shouting for the sheriff in the background and the faint wail of approaching sirens. "I've got to run y'all. Just come by the office on your way in." the sheriff said followed by an abrupt ending of the call.

The highway from Nashville seemed never-ending; it was a long drive into nothingness. They had long since lost cell service and no longer had the ability to stream music to pass the time. Beside the occasional bit of road noise or a random snore from Brit, the ride had grown silent. "Ok, I need some noise, even if it's some bull shit country-bumpkin radio station!" Elijah belted out to the group, waking Brit from her nap. "I don't think I know how to turn on the radio," Tristan said laughingly. "I don't think I've ever used it," he continued with a chuckle. Elijah fiddled with the buttons on the dash until he discovered the loud roar of radio static. He spun the knobs round and round looking for any signs of life from the FM stations. Only discovering more static, he firmly pressed the "AM" button and continued his search for life. A loud voice cackled over the stereo as he tuned past it; he quickly turned the knob back and honed in on the station. *"This is WBRK 540 AM – Lola's source for music, sports, and news!"* the enthusiastic broadcaster said through the radio. Some modern non-descript canned country song began playing; after a few more generic *Top 40* hits the DJ was back. *"This is a WBRK 540 breaking news story!"* the DJ excitedly said. Tristan leaned forward and turned up the volume on the stereo.

"We're receiving initial reports of police, fire, and ems activity at Lake View Park in our sister to the east, Langford. Let's cut to a local reporter on the scene, Jenifer Hempstead. Jenifer?"

"Hello Rick, we're here at Lake View Park in Lanford. There is a lot of police presence at the moment along with units from local fire and ems departments. It looks like there are rescuers in the water at this very moment.

Most emergency personal are being very tight lipped, but one did mention that they were called out for an unresponsive person in the water. The presence of the county coroner makes this appear to be more of a recovery than a rescue. We'll keep our eye on the situation as this story develops. Back to you Rick."

"Prayers for all those involved and our brave first responders. The potential for a grim outcome seems high but let's hope things turn out positively. We'll check back in with Jenifer in a bit for new developments. This is WBRK 540 AM."

Pop country soon filled the car once again; the group sat quietly trying to process exactly what they had heard. In a futile attempt to calm the nerves of his friends, Elijah said, "I'm sure it's nothing." He continued, "There is no way that this has anything to do with Hunter." No one responded, they all sat quietly on edge waiting for more news from the radio station. Bad news always travels fast, the friends didn't have to wait long for an update on the situation transpiring at Lake View. As yet another country hit wound down to a close, the radio DJ was back with his deep radio voice.

"This is WBRK 540 AM – Lola's source for music, sports, and news! We're continuing to follow the developing story out of Langford. There is an active emergency situation at Lake View Park that has resulted in sizable police, fire and ems response. I understand that we have an update from our correspondent on the scene. Let's head back over to Jenifer Hempstead, Jenifer?"

"A macabre sight here at Lake View, Rick. Police have confirmed that they received a call about an hour ago for an unresponsive person in the water. Upon on responding to the scene they discovered that there was a deceased white male appearing to be between 30 and 40 years of age floating near the swimming area of Lake View. They currently have retrieved the body from the water and are transporting this individual to the coroner's office in Lola. A source close to the sheriff's office had indicated that this appears to be a suicide as the remnants of a note were discovered along with the body. This is all obviously preliminary information and is subject to change as this story continues to unfold. No matter the cause, we can confirm one dead a Lake View Park. This is a sad day for all of the residents of

Langford. We'll keep you updated as we discover more. Back to you Rick."

"A sad day indeed Jenifer. Let's keep this person, their family, and friends in our thoughts and prayers. A huge thank you to all of our local first responders for your service to this community and all of its residents. This is WBRK 540!"

The group sat in a state of shock from what they had just heard. "Could this really be Hunter?" Elijah thought to himself as Tristan angrily turn off the radio. Tristan could sense Elijah's worry and grasped his hand tightly. Brit never uttered a word; her usual loud demeanor had been silenced by the disturbing report. While Tristan and Elijah remained hopeful that this was not connected to Hunters disappearance, Brit was certain that it was. She knew in her gut that this was Hunter, she knew that she had lost one of her adopted wayward children. She could feel the loss in her bones; her motherly inclination towards the boys granted her the ability to feel his loss. She could feel it long before she even knew that it was him.

The room was strange; it felt so foreign to those that had never witnessed the underlying mechanics of death firsthand. The rooms utilitarian appearance only made it seem that much more bizarre. There was tile covering the floor and running half-way up each wall, two large swinging metal doors served as its only entry and exit point, the big square tiled room was lined with large metal and glass cabinets, various pieces of archaic appearing pseudo-medical tools and apparatus were scattered about the various counters, and three large metal tables graced the center of the space. The smell of formaldehyde and decay hung in the cold stale air of the room; it was like staring death in the face. "I need to warn you about what you're about to see." Sheriff

Morales said to Elijah, Tristan, and Brit, snapping them out of a daze. Prior to finding themselves in the alien-like setting of the county morgue, they had made their way to the sheriff's office. The sheriff had informed them that he believed the body recovered from Lake View was Hunters. Upon hearing the news, no one spoke a word. Each stared blankly through the sheriff standing before them, the blood drained from their skin, and each let out an audible groan of disbelief. Sheriff Morales had seen this look hundreds, if not thousands, of times throughout his career. Sheriff Morales knew death well, but he never expected death to follow him to the sleepy County of Watkins, Tennessee. Prior to escorting them to the morgue, the sheriff had informed the group that they had recovered some personal belongings from the body and needed them to see if this person was, in fact, Hunter. Their somber agreement had now led them into the belly of the Watkins County Morgue.

"Did you hear what I said?" Sheriff Morales asked. "This is not going to be easy," he said. "There's no nice way to put this, the body has been in the water for a few days and nature has started to take it's course. The body is in rough shape." He continued in an effort to prepare the trio for the grim sight that awaited them across the room. Elijah peered around the sheriff at one of the metal tables in the center of the room; a lumpy and lifeless body-shaped object laid atop the cold metal table and was draped in a stained white sheet. The reality of what he was about to see crippled Elijah; he was paralyzed by the thought that the lifeless thing could be Hunter. A small, gray-haired woman in light-blue scrubs then entered the room. The loud squeaky swinging doors made her presence known and broke Elijah's trance-like fixation with the corpse across the room. She made her way to a rack of medical coats and gowns next to a desk; she immediately started donning medical garb and made her way towards the sheriff. "Did you warn them?" she asked of Sheriff Morales. "As best as I could," he muttered in response. "I'm sorry about all this," the woman said in an empathetic tone as she turned to greet the group of friends. "I'm Doctor Hale, I'm the medical examiner for the county. Well, Watkins County and about three others. Small town life…" She said while extending her hand to shake each members of the group. "Follow me," she then said while making her way towards one of the counters lining the wall of the morgue.

She tore the top off of a dark-brown paper bag that was sealed shut with red tape that read: "EVIDENCE." She carefully retrieved the bags contents one by one, placing each out on the silver metallic countertop for the group to examine. Piece by piece, she laid out a slim leather wallet, a keyring with a *Mercedes* car key and various other keys, a wound-up pair of earbuds, a leather belt, a plastic baggy containing a small amount of waterlogged marijuana, a gold *Zippo* lighter bearing the likeness of Buddha, and some loose change. Elijah recoiled upon viewing the items; he was thrown for a loop. Tristan grabbed him in an embrace as they both instantly recognized several of the items. Brit continued to stare down at the items in disbelief as the medical examiner started to open the wallet. "Hunter Howell, born February 21st, 1986, resided at 1674 West Hickory Street in Nashville, Tennessee, organ donor," the doctor read aloud in a monotone voice. "Can you confirm if any or all of these items belonged to your friend?" she asked of the group abruptly. "It's him, it's his stuff," Brit said breaking her silence and beginning to weep. "Thank you dear," the medical examiner said while gently touching her shoulder to comfort her. "One more step, please follow me," she then said as the doctor made her way towards the ominous object under the stained white sheet across the room. The broken and reeling friends slowly congregated around what appeared to be the head of the lifeless corpse. The sheriff stood behind them, somberly staring down at the mirror-like shine of his black shoes. The sheriff knew what came next; it was the worst part of his career choice. As the sheet was pulled downward, Brit let out a blood-curdling scream and stepped backwards in horror. Sheriff Morales was waiting to comfort her upon the revelation that Hunter was no more. Even though she had known that Hunter was gone since the very first radio broadcast, seeing his lifeless face solidified the nightmare. Elijah grabbed at Tristan in search of his hand, finally finding it and grasping it tightly. Tristan reciprocated his squeeze by squeezing back that much harder. Tristan and Elijah both stared down at a cold, bloated, lifeless Hunter Howell. His skin looked loose and slippery, his pale milky eyes peered into the ceiling above him, and he appeared bruised and scrapped. He was Hunter, but he wasn't the Hunter that they all once knew. "That's him," Elijah said raspingly while trying to catch his breath. "That's our friend Hunter," he said.

The cold formaldehyde-soaked air of the morgue was soon replaced with the burnt coffee smell of Sheriff Morales's office. Strangely enough, the dark and bitterly strong coffee the Sheriff made for the group was the most comforting thing they had experienced so far that day. "If you're ever in a new town and can't find good coffee, just swing by the police station or a firehouse;" the sheriff said in his deep and gruff tone. "Just tell them I sent you," he continued. For all of his goodness and professional ability, certain social graces were lost on the calloused lawman. As good as a person as he was, when and where to insert humor was lost on him. "Suicide?" Brit said aloud to no one in particular. "There's no way Sheriff, Hunter was not like that," Elijah chimed in corroborating Brits disbelief of what they had heard through the radio on the way into town. "Hunter is a lot of things, but listen, he was way too fond of himself to ever hurt himself, there's no way!" Tristan stated joining his friends in disbelief. "Suicide? Where in God's name did you hear that?" the sheriff responded puzzled. "What? The radio!" Brit aggressively shouted. "They said that sources close to the Sheriffs Offices indicated that it was suicide," Tristan went on to explain as Brit was overcome with anger. Sheriff Morales looked up at the yellowing paint of the ceiling above him in disbelief. "How in the God damn hell does everyone else know more about what's going on here than I do?" he shouted in anger. He stood from his desk abruptly and made his way towards the window across the room. He stared out into the parking lot silently, attempting to cool his anger and collect his thoughts. "What the fuck is going on," he muttered to himself. "Someone is trying to burry this," he continued as he thought out loud to himself. "Who would want to make this go way," he stated as he tried to formulate his thoughts.

After a few long minutes of silence, Sheriff Morales made his way back to his desk and set down. "Remember when I said this situation stays between us?" the sheriff asked of the trio of friends. They all nodded back at him agreement. "Keep it that way," he said firmly. "Your friend did not kill himself; someone is fucking around," he informed the group while speaking at a near whisper. "I've never seen a suicidal person beat the dog piss out of themselves, shoot themselves in the back of the head, and then dump their own body in a lake!" he said while dipping back into his anger of what was transpiring in his sleepy little county. "I've known Jane, the medical examiner, a long time.

She's an outsider like me, like you three," he said. "She deals only in facts; she's not concerned with the politics or beliefs of this place" he continued on to say while tapping on the medical examiner's report that laid on top of his desk. "This report goes on to say that there were post-mortem ligature marks around Hunters ankles that contained small bits of fibers consistent with rope. I'm no genius, but it looks like he was weighted down. Whoever did this thought the lake would hide the truth for years to come." Sheriff Morales explained. "What about the note?" Brit asked inquisitively. "Let me guess? A source close to the Sheriffs Office?" the sheriff replied sarcastically. The group again nodded at the sheriff in agreement. "That's pure bull shit! The only items recovered from the scene are the ones that you took a look at in the morgue." He continued. "Stay close and keep quiet, I'll be touch soon," the sheriff said while opening the door to indicate that the interview was over. "I need to get to work," Sheriff Morales said to the group as they departed his office.

The aroma of Ruby's home cooking did nothing to ease the nerves of the friends; the smell of morgue and decay still permeated their nostrils. They were gathered around Ruby's kitchen table; the same table they had unknowingly shared with Hunter for his last meal just days ago. They each again thanked Aunt Ruby for her gracious hospitality as they pushed the food around their plates as to keep up the appearance of eating. "I'm so sorry children," Ruby said to the group. "Though we sometimes do not understand, it's all part of God plan," she continued. The religious nature of her comments only served to further dampen the friend's moods. "Well fuck god and fuck his plan!" Elijah thought to himself in response; a blasphemous thought that he would dare never utter aloud to Ruby. "Oh, and I've asked pastor, Seth, and some of the others from the church to swing by later just incase y'all would like to talk." Ruby said as she made her way from the kitchen and towards her recliner in the living room. "Great news guys, they're going to pray the sadness out of us! Then they'll have god swoop down and find the piece of shit that killed Hunter," Brit whispered to Elijah and Tristan from across the table.

  Soon the house was filled with the light chatter of various conversations. The smell of food again flooded the home; food brought along by the crowd of church goers. In the small town of Langford, like many others scattered across the country, death was always followed by various covered dishes and fried chicken. It reminded Elijah of his first "fellowship" at the Second Coming Church. He saw many familiar faces and shook many familiar hands. All the attendees presented him and his friends with the same or similar near-scripted questions and responses: "How are you?" or "Are you ok?" and Elijah's least favorite, "I'm so sorry for your loss." As Elijah, Tristan, and Brit, set in the kitchen, their mourning now a public spectacle for the congregation of the Second Coming Bible Church, Randy Ward and Seth caught his eye. Seth's masculine southern charm had drawn Elijah's gaze prior, but this was different. Seth's body language had shifted; he was in a deep conversation with Randy and appeared to be distraught. Elijah had never seen Seth disheveled, other than when he noticed his torn shirt at the diner. Seth was always calm, charming, and well put together. He took note of how the pair seemed to argue back and forth, waving their arms around wildly at one another. Seth soon noticed Elijah's stare and quickly motioned to Randy to calm down, drawing Randy's attention to Elijah's watchful eye. Seth left his emotional conversation with Randy to make his way towards the friends. But, before Seth could make his way to Elijah, Sheriff Morales had arrived at Ruby's and found the trio of friends. "We need to talk," the sheriff said as he leaned down toward the friends and motioned towards the kitchen door.

Before the sheriff could say anything, Elijah mentioned Seth and Randy's odd conversation. "It was just strange; they were arguing back and forth, and I just have a bad feeling about it." Elijah blurted out to the sheriff. "Seth seemed a little off at the diner the other day..." Tristan then added to Elijah's concerned comments. "You noticed that, too?" Elijah asked of Tristan as he turned towards him. "Yeah, Brit and I even talked about it, but I didn't want you to think that I was just being jealous, so I didn't say anything." Tristan explained. "He just seemed off," Brit added to Tristan's explanation. "Seth, huh?" the sheriff asked after a few minutes of fighting to get a word in. "Let's pause that for just a moment so I can fill you in on what I've found so far," the sheriff then stated to quiet the group. "I've pulled Hunter's phone records and his bank statements; I had an old judge friend that owed me a favor and he quietly helped me out with a warrant," the crafty lawman said. "The last activity on his phone, was the message he sent to Elijah, but his bank statements are another story entirely." Sheriff Morales continued. "There have been three charges since Hunters presumed time of death. One at The Speedy Spot Gas Station for $32.75 and two at King Kongs Kones for a about $20 bucks each. Unfortunately, neither location has cameras. Security isn't really a thing they do around these parts." The sheriff continued to explain. "At the Speedy Spot, the card was used at the pump on the morning of Hunters disappearance. As for King Kongs, it was used later that same day and again just two days ago." Sheriff Morales said. "I also went back to Lake View to poke around for myself. That park is the only real access to the water, so if one wanted to dump something in the water, they would have to do it there." the sheriff explained. "Thanks to our recent spell of good weather, the area is still quite well preserved. I found what appeared to be drag marks down the trail, some bits of hair consistent with Hunter's, and a scrap of red and black fabric stuck to a thorn bush." The sheriff concluded.

Elijah's brain was working at a feverish pace to connect all of the dots that Sheriff Morales had laid out before him and his friends. The epiphany that struck Elijah was almost audible; the seemingly meaningless scraps of information suddenly snapped together in his mind. On the day that Hunter had disappeared, the friends were at King Kong's Kones; they were there again just two days ago. Both of these days, they had seen Seth there as well. On both of these days, someone had used Hunters bank card. The red and black scrap of fabric the sheriff found, the same scrap the trio had noticed the first time they had explored Lake View, matched Seth's torn red and black flannel shirt. Seth somehow had found himself at all the right places; Seth's southern charm could no longer explain away these coincidences. Elijah poured out these revelations to his friend and the sheriff, each coming to the same conclusion as Elijah. Seth was somehow involved in what happened to their friend; Seth knew something about Hunter.

Elijah had pieced together the facts that Sheriff Morales could not, but the sharp lawman had yet more to reveal. "Deputy Randy Ward…" the sheriff uttered. "…I have a lot of suspicion and some proof that he's involved as well." The sheriff continued. "He purposely flubbed the report and has actively attempted to keep this whole thing quiet." The sheriff explained. "I asked him about Hunters phone, and he indicated that it wasn't recovered. He approached Jane about her findings from the autopsy and tried to persuade her that Hunter was a suicide," the sheriff said. "A source close to *WBRK 540*..." the gruff sheriff said with a proud chuckle, "informed me that Randy Ward was their source that was close to the Sheriff's Office." He continued. The sheriff was never very fond of Deputy Randy Ward; he was a lazy police officer and lackluster on his best days. Jackson Morales could deal with lazy, but Randy was also sloppy, an outlaw, and loved to pick fights. Randy was born and raised in Langford; he was reborn and raised again at the Second Coming Bible Church during his teenage years. After finding God and graduating Lanford high, Randy joined the *Marines* and found himself serving multiple back-to-back tours in the first and second Gulf Wars. Randy had developed a near bloodlust while fighting overseas, a bloodlust he brought with him back to Langford. When the *Marines* would no longer have him, Randy packed up and headed home. Upon his return he was hired by his uncle, an uncle who was then the Sheriff of Watkins County. Nepotism, rather than skill or desire, afforded Randy a job as an officer of the law. Sheriff Morales distained Randy, how he procured his job, and all that he stood for. His religious extremism, coupled with his rageful desires, would result in him preaching to a suspect one moment and cracking them in the head with a baton the next. Randy Ward was a predator of the worst kind; a predator who believed that God was on his side.

Sheriff Jackson Morales had the ability to discern facts from feelings; he acquired this skill through his numerous years as a professional lawman. All of his personal feeling aside, the facts fit together seamlessly. The group of friends, along with Sheriff Morales, now knew that Seth and Randy were somehow involved with Hunter's murder. But to what extent was lost on them; the two had not even met Hunter. Did they know Hunter? Did they kill him? Even with the group's newfound revelations, there seemed to be more questions than answers. If one deputy were involved, could there be more? How does Seth fit into this, and more importantly, how do Seth and Randy fit in this together? An even grander and looming question also exists, why? Why would anyone, much less two men from the sleepy little town of Langford, want a man that neither of them knew dead? Why would they kill Hunter? The group could feel the peering eyes of the congregation beginning to burn into their skin; a small watch-party had formed at the window to observe them chatting in the backyard. "Looks like we have company. Fucking small town life..." the sheriff said while motioning towards the window with a quick glance. Now speaking loud enough for the gawkers to hear, the sharp-witted sheriff said, "I'm so sorry for your loss, it's really a tragic thing. Suicide is never an easy thing to accept, if you need someone to talk to, we have counselors available through the sheriff's office. I'm always here for you kids as well, I'll check on you soon." The sheriff then shook their hands, tipped his dark-brown cap at the crowd of onlookers, and made his through a side gate and towards his black patrol car.

The friends could take no more of this public spectacle; they couldn't muster an ounce of desire to go back in that house. The circus of revelers, each spewing insincere messages of hope and God, was all too much to handle. The eating and drinking, the festivities of death in the south, turned their stomachs and their minds ill. Tristan could sense that Elijah was unraveling, grabbing him by the arm he said to Elijah and Brit, "Let's get out of here for a bit?" They were all silent as Tristan drove them in circles around Langford; they were each trying to process the discoveries that they had made about Hunter, Seth, and Randy. Soon enough, they found themselves on that rural forest road towards

Lake View. Elijah, realizing where they were, said to Tristan, "pull into the park? I'm tired of driving in circles but don't want to go back to Ruby's yet." Tristan said nothing in response, but silently agreed by slowly turning into the parking lot. He cautiously avoided the series of potholes at the park's entrance, and parked the vehicle overlooking the sandy beach area where they had once visited. The sun was setting over the lake, it would soon be night. Brit remarked on the fiery beauty of the sunset, but quickly mentioned how her memory of the area's natural beauty would forever be stained by the death of Hunter. "Hunter would have hated this," Elijah blurted out laughingly. The friends all chuckled out loud at the truthfulness of Elijah's comment about the sunset. "That he would have, babe." Tristan replied while reaching for Elijah's hand. Brit turned from her seat and began rummaging around in the expansive cargo area of the big SUV. After a few minutes of searching she exclaimed, "Ah ha! Found you!" as she pulled the half-full bottle of *Jägermeister* from behind the seat.

"Ugh that's nasty!" Tristan shouted after taking a large swig from the bottle and placing it on the hood of his car. "Hunter would have hated you for bringing this nasty shit, Brit!" he then blurted out. "Do you remember the last time we had *Jägermeister*?" Brit asked of the two men. Elijah instantly recoiled in embarrassment; he had heard this story hundreds of times before. "Yeah, I do," Tristan said with a loud laugh and a glance in Elijah's direction. "I remember you and me having to carry this one and Hunter out of what seemed like every bar in Nashville, we had to keep them from going to jail at an IHOP, and then we had to tuck them in at your place after they both got sick!" Tristan said replying to Brit. "You get sloppy one time and you never live it down," Elijah shouted back at them. "That was actually a really fun night," Brit said trying to curb Elijah's embarrassment. "I would give anything to get to have that night again." She continued. Brit quickly countered her somber comment with another embarring moment from that night in Nashville. "Oh! Oh! Oh!" she shouted. "I also remember you professing your undying love for this one that night, too" Brit laughingly said to Elijah while motioning towards Tristan with her eyes. Elijah had loved Tristan long before he would ever admit it to himself, much less anyone else. Alcohol had diminished his ability to hide his love any longer, at least for that night in Nashville. "I did do that, huh?" Elijah said with a chuckle. "I did, and I meant it," he said while eyeing Tristan. Their conversation soon fell silent as their words were replaced with the sounds of the surrounding forest. They each silently reminisced about their own individual memories of their friend Hunter Howell.

Hunter might have been the newest member to join the small tight-knit group, but you would have never known. To an outsider, one would believe this mismatched little group of friends had known each other their entire lives, but that would be far from the truth. Over his first three months in Nashville, Elijah met Brit, Tristan, and then Hunter. Soon, they would all be inseparable. Hunter Howell was typically a quiet man, usually only opening his mouth to insert a smart-ass comment or a mind-blowing piece of wisdom into a conversation. He was intelligent beyond belief, he was "book smart" along with being full of "whisky wisdom," he liked video games, he liked smoking pot, he had a great career, and he loved his friends deeply. His deep level of love for his friend was compounded by the fact that he had no real family to speak of. Hunter grew up in the system after being nearly beaten to death by his abusive mother at the age of 7; he lived most of his life as an outcast until he found Elijah. Hunter

Howell had a good heart; a good heart he hid behind his "ass hole" persona. Hunter had developed this uncaring and calloused façade as a defense during his time as a foster kid, a shield that he carried with him into adulthood. When Elijah met Hunter, he could see through his act, he could see the true man behind the disguise. Hunter feared rejection more than everything else, he was perpetually single, choosing the life of a bachelor over the chance that someone might break his heart. Hunter didn't need love, all Hunter needed was Elijah, Tristan, and Brit. All Hunter truly had in life was Elijah, Tristan, and Brit.

After several more throat burning swigs from the dark-green bottle of alcohol, a few tears, a lot of laughs, and story after story about Hunter, it was time to call it night. A short drive across Langford led the half-drunk group of mourning friends back to Aunt Ruby's; they each busied themselves with their normal nighttime rituals as they prepared for bed. "Are you sure we can't sleep together?" Tristan asked of Elijah as he stood in the doorway of Elijah's room. Elijah's face drooped in sadness as he responded to Tristan's request, "We can't risk Aunt Ruby knowing," he explained. "What's she going to do? Beat us with a bible?" Tristan asked sarcastically. "Babe..." Elijah muttered as he tried to formulate a response to Tristan's well-justified frustration. "You have to come at some point Elijah! We have to come out at some point!" Tristan whispered angrily in Elijah's direction. The stress from the situation, and the tragedy of Hunters young life being cut short, had led Tristan to re-evaluate what was truly important in his life. Elijah's rejection of him in this moment, coupled with the grim situation at hand, had pushed Tristan to his boiling point. Even though it had taken years, Tristan now realized that Elijah was the most important thing to him. "Just not now," Elijah said defeatedly. "Let's figure out what happened to Hunter first, and then we'll never have to think about this backwoods place, it's backwoods beliefs, or Aunt Ruby ever again." Elijah concluded. Tristan walked over to Elijah, kissed him, and left the room shaking his head in disappointment.

Elijah tossed and turned, wrapping himself tighter and tighter in the homemade quilt on top on the old squeaky antique guest bed. Elijah was again engulfed by nightmares, calling for hunter into the black void that surround him. He again found himself in the forest that surrounds Lake View, he again found himself screaming out to Aunt Ruby, he again witnessed her pull Hunters bloated corpse from the near-black waters of the lake, he again heard her speak words from the bible, and he again woke gasping for air and screaming Ruby's name. Elijah set up in the bed, still reeling from the horrific nightmare. He set there for what felt like hours; he could not sleep after again experiencing the morbid visions that now seemed to plague him endlessly. He peered across the room to a glowing red blob in the corner. As his eyes focused, he could make out the time on the black and faux wood ancient looking clock, it read 3:45 AM. A loud rumble suddenly emitted from Elijah's belly, after not eating all day, his appetite had finally caught up to him. He stumbled around aimlessly in the dark in search of his shirt, finally finding it at the foot of the bed. He then tiptoed down the hall and past his friends that were sleeping in adjacent rooms. With each step, the 100-year-old floors groaned and screamed under his weight. He carefully made his way down the steps and into the kitchen in search of food. As he pulled open the fridge door, he could see dishes covered in tinfoil stacked to the top of the antique refrigerator. After grabbing a fork from a nearby drawer and a random dish from the fridge, he took a seat at the empty kitchen table.

Elijah ate until he could eat no more; his now bloated belly pushed lightly against the kitchen table. He had no clue what he had eaten, but it fulfilled his bodies raging hunger. As he set there in the dimly lit kitchen, staring at an empty casserole dish, a picture from the living room caught his attention. He stood up from the table and began wandering towards it. It was a picture of him and his mother from when he was growing up in South Carolina; the picture set atop an aged wooden cabinet in a dated ornate gold frame. Elijah took a moment to admire the pictures reminiscent quality, it took him back to a much simpler time while growing up in rural South Carolina. Soon he found himself observing many of the numerous other old pictures and artifacts that lined every inch of the historic homestead; Elijah felt as if he were a casual observer at a museum. Looking soon turned to exploring as Elijah began peaking into drawers and opening up random cabinets and boxes that appeared interesting to him. He discovered drawers full of family pictures, prehistoric church literature and pamphlets, bible after bible, bits of old loose jewelry and coins, and a mountain of small worthless trinkets that his Aunt Ruby had collected over her life. Elijah was excavating through Ruby's life; a sleep deprived archeologist digging into the past to cure his boredom and to feed his curious nature. Inside of the old wooden cabinet, the one with the picture of him and his mother, he found a worn carboard box. Inside of this box he found a small wooden jewelry box with a cross carved into its top. Elijah held the box up to his ear and gave it a light shake to see if it held any treasure; the box gave a light "clunk" in response to his efforts. He flipped up the box's small brass latch, opened its lid, and gazed down in disbelief. Inside of the small-wooden container was a shattered cell phone; Ruby had Hunter's cell phone.

In a panicked state of fear and disbelief, Elijah slammed the small-wooden box shut and shoved it deeply back into the weathered cardboard box from which he discovered it. Grasping Hunter's damaged phone in his hands, he swiftly surveyed all the areas that he had explored to ensure that all was left exactly how he found it. After shoving the phone into the waistband of his underwear, he moved fast to clean up the remnants of his early morning feast. He washed and put away the casserole dish, he washed and placed his fork back into its rightful place, and he wiped down any crumbs or splatter he left on the kitchen table. Elijah then silently retraced his footsteps from the kitchen to his bedroom. He slowly shut and locked the door, crawled back into the old squeaky bed, wrapped himself up in the old thick colorful quilt, and then retrieved the phone from his waistband. "Hunter..." Elijah muttered to himself in a continued state of disbelief. "Why would Aunt Ruby have you?" he asked, questioning the damaged cell phone. Elijah stared blankly at the phone in his hands until shards of sunlight began reflecting from its shattered screen and into his eye. The sun was breaking through the window behind him, he glanced at the glowing red clock once again – 6:02 AM. Elijah shoved Hunters phone between the mattress and box spring, finally laying his head again on the cool pillow behind him. As quickly as Elijah had laid down, the noise of an approaching car forced him to again rise. The clanky puttering of the vehicle and squealing brakes sounded familiar; the rumbling noise soon ceased and was followed by the groaning sound of the old homes screen door opening and closing. He soon could hear muffled voices beyond the closed window of his bedroom. Elijah's curious nature and his need for answers forced him to look; he could see Ruby greeting Granny Jean Ward in the driveway. Ruby, in her current state of frailty, had managed to meet her halfway. Elijah, cautiously gazing at them from behind the curtain, also noticed a familiar truck with a familiar face in its driver's seat. It was Seth Nelson.

With a light "Click," Elijah unlocked the bedroom window. Pushing forcefully, yet slowly upwards, he cracked the window just enough the hear the exchange below him. "Come, let's chat up on the porch?" he heard his aunt ask of Granny Jean. "I guess I can sit a spell," he heard the old woman respond. Watching closely, he could see the woman's bright-white cotton-like hair disappear under the porches roof; Seth remained patiently in the rusty white truck in the driveway. "I'm worried Jean…" he heard Ruby say. "Why did you choose him?" she asked of the church elder. "I didn't choose anyone!" Granny Jean quickly responded. "God does all the choosing in our church," Granny continued on to state in a stern tone. Aunt Ruby now remained silent, listening to what Granny Jean had to say. "And as for that boy, he's as good as any. If anything, the church gave him a gift! He was given the gift of mercy, the gift of helping to fulfill God's word, and the gift of fulling God's works through this church!" Aunt Ruby continued to express her concern with the happenings around town, in particular, all of the attention Hunter's death was receiving. "God help me, I'm still worried Jean. This could be the undoing of all we've worked towards," Ruby said. "Have faith Ruby, God has a plan. God's plan, along with a little help from Randy and Seth, can't be stopped," Granny jean replied. As the two women said their goodbyes, Elijah slowly closed the window and relatched it. He pushed Hunters cell phone deeper under the mattress for good measure, and then slid back into the now cold blankets of the bed. He again heard the groan of the opening and closing of the screen door. It was soon followed by the metallic clanks of pots and pans in the kitchen; Aunt Ruby would soon have breakfast on the table for the trio of friends.

Lake View Park's natural beauty was in stark contrast to the haunting image of Hunters bloated corpse that was now seared into Elijah's mind. The impact of this grim image had only been compounded by Elijah's vivid and graphic night terrors. Elijah, Tristan, and Brit found themselves at the lakeside park awaiting the arrival of Sheriff Morales. Elijah had just confessed all of the disturbing details about what he had witnessed earlier this same morning; he had revealed the discovery of Hunters phone that he had found hidden at Aunt Ruby's. The car was filled with a mixture of panicked fear and anger. "I'm going to fuck her up!" Brit shouted enraged from the backseat. "That old bitch knows something and I'm going to find out what it is!" she continued to say in her state of panic. "Just wait on the sheriff," Tristan said calmy in response to Brits growing anger. Elijah, fighting back the same anger and confusion that Brit was experiencing, forced himself to side with Tristan. Tristan was right, nothing good could come from the group galivanting around like a ragtag gang of vigilantes. "Sheriff Morales will know what to do Brit," Elijah said in a calm and confident manner. Elijah had been afforded a longer amount of time to think; he had time to process some of his boiling rage and confusion. He had been forced to face Ruby that morning at breakfast, he had been forced to put on a fake smile as she served him her homemade biscuits and gravy, and he had been forced to hug her goodbye as the friends left for the park. Elijah had grown accustom to hiding in plain sight, a skill he acquired over the years of grappling with his sexual identity in small town America. But much like in his personal life, how long could he keep this up? "How could Aunt Ruby be involved? Why would she be involved?" Elijah thought to himself as he sat in the void of silence that had crept into the car. The young man knew his Aunt Ruby, but he admittedly didn't know Ruby all that well. "There's just no way..." he silently said in his mind as he continued to patiently wait for the Sheriff and ponder on the mystery.

Elijah had never been that close with Ruby; he was never very close with any of his family for that matter. The Howard and Morgan clans were scattered across the country and the family did not keep in touch regularly. With many of his relatives residing far from the little South Carolina town where Elijah had spent most of his life, communication was infrequent at best. Elijah's father, Henry Howard, had died just before Elijah's second birthday. Henry Howard had been an iron worker and that job ultimately cost him his life. Elijah had heard the story of his father's tragic industrial demise a handful of times throughout his youth from his mother. The young man only knew his dad through faded pictures plastered in his mother's photo albums and short stories that his mother would share with him from time to time. Elijah and his mother had moved to rural South Carolina not long after his father's death; he could not remember a time before living in his little southern hometown. According to his mother, while she was growing up in a small town near Langford, she had met his father. They quickly became romantic and the young lovers were soon blessed with a child; Elijah Howard was a natural born Tennessean. After spending the first two years of his existence in rural Tennessee, he spent the next 20 years or so of his life in South Carolina before migrating back to the volunteer state. Over the years, he had only met Ruby twice, both times at family reunions his mother had forced him to attend. He knew his mother's sister more through her recollections, than his own firsthand experiences. Beyond her love of Jesus, cheesecake, and menthol cigarettes, Elijah didn't know much about Ruby. In all actuality, Elijah didn't know Ruby at all.

Elijah was on edge; he had now grown suspicious of all those that were involved with the Second Coming Bible Church. Elijah was fearful of Ruby, Granny Jean, Seth, Randy, and the entire congregation of the small backwoods church. Elijah's fear was only trumped by his growing suspicion and confusion about Ruby and the churches involvement; but why? "Why?" A question that continued to plague the now incomplete little group of friends; this unanswered question was echoing through each of their heads. Elijah's lack of knowledge about Ruby was not lost on him, his ignorance of who the old dying woman was, only served to incite his fear and suspicion more. Elijah had spent his remaining time in bed that morning considering confronting her, but his fear crippled him. He kept asking himself, "if they did this to Hunter, would they do the same to the rest of us?" In these early morning hours, he realized that Sheriff Morales was their only hope. The calloused old lawman was the only person that could solve hunters murder and get them out of Langford unscathed. After forcing himself from bed that morning, he individually asked Brit and Tristan if they could drive out to the lake. While hiding in the bathroom across the hallway from his room, he called Sheriff Morales to set up the meeting. Elijah Howard then put on his fake smile and made his way to breakfast.

A jet-black shiny Impala backed in swiftly beside of Tristan's big black SUV. As both the Sheriff and the friends exited their vehicles, the sheriff laughed loudly and yelled, "Well damn, we'd better be careful! Folks will start thinking the FBI's here if they see all of these new black cars rolling around together." The sheriffs lighthearted comments were only a cover to protect the friends from how worrisome the situation actually made him. "Get in!" he shouted as he set back down in his new police cruiser. The group drove out of the park and turned away from the town of Langford once they met the forest highway. Elijah explained in detail to the sheriff all that he had witnessed earlier in the day. He handed Sheriff Morales Hunter's cell phone and explained how he had discovered it at Ruby's. He opened up to the lawman about his now burning suspicions about his aunt and the church she served. The sheriff remained quiet as he listened attentively; he was diligently connecting the dots within his crime-solving mind. Sheriff Morales then abruptly and simultaneously slammed on the brakes, turned on his emergency lights, and chirped the car's siren a few times while pulling a U-turn between oncoming traffic. He then turned off the lights and drove regularly. Seeing the look of shock on the friends faces, he said with a laugh, "perk of the job!" while he continued to chuckle for a few moments after the humorous comment. Still confused by the sudden turn back towards Langford, Sheriff Morales offered some of an explanation. "We need to go see someone." He said while picking up speed towards Langford.

As they emerged from the thick forest highway, Langford lay dead ahead. "I didn't think I could hate this place worse than when I first arrived, but I proved myself wrong." Elijah thought to himself as they neared the tiny little town. The sheriff passed King Kong's Kones, then the Speedy Spot, then the half-empty strip mall, then the Second Coming Bible Church, and then the vehicle came to a stop in front of a big metal building. Elijah recognized where they were, they had arrived at the Christ Almighty Worship Center. "They are friends, trust me?" The sheriff said sensing the trio's confusion. If the group had ill-feelings about religion before their time in Lanford, it could only be described as hatred now. As the sheriff exited the car, the three friends cautiously followed behind him. The sheriff pushed on the door bearing a large black hand painted cross and stepped into the church. After a moment of brief hesitation, the friends followed him inside. Despite its industrial exterior, the interior of the Christ Almighty Worship Center was quite modern and well appointed. Everything seemed clean and new; the atmosphere felt light and welcoming. The Christ Almighty Worship Center was worlds apart from the Second Coming Bible Church. Pastor Bill Hall quickly greeted the group, "Come in, come in," he shouted as he made his way towards the small crowd of people gathered by the entrance. He shook each of their hands and welcomed them into the church. "Come on this way, let's head down to my office." He said as he motioned for the group to follow him down a nearby set of stairs.

The pastor's office was neat, tidy, and well kept. The shelves lining its walls bore mementos and photographs from the pastor's global travels and charitable works. A new computer graced his large ornate desk and a large flat-screen television hung on the adjacent wall. The pastor was a man of God, but he was a modern man of God. "So, what's happened now?" the friendly pastor asked of Sheriff Morales. The sheriff explained the interaction that Elijah had witnessed earlier in the day and revealed the discovery of the cell phone; Elijah inserted various missed details and corrections as the sheriff told his story. Brit, now growing impatient, interrupted the conversation by shouting, "what the fuck are we doing here?" Her profane comment made no impact on the pastor; Bill Hall glanced in her direction with an understanding gaze and said "Sheriff?" Sheriff Morales explained to the group of friends that Pastor Bill was aware of the details of the case and had some of his own information to share. "I've been watching Second Coming for a while now," the pastor began. "They are up to no good," he then said. "Religion aside, there is good and evil in this world. When you add God to good, things often become great. When you add God to evil, it brings about the worst in humanity, it brings about hell itself." The pastor rattled off in an ominous tone. "The Second Coming Bible Church is more of an extremist cult than a church," the pastor concluded as he stood from his desking and started digging through a large metal filling cabinet behind him. Pastor Bill Hall was well acquainted with cults and extreme beliefs; he had dedicated much of his career to studying them and extinguishing them from the world. This mission to eradicate this evil had taken him all over the globe; this mission is what ultimately brought him to Langford. After finding several manila folders he then turned and handed them to Elijah. "It's all in there" he said. "I just didn't realize just how extreme they had become," the pastor said while shaking his head in disgust.

Before Elijah could open the folders, there was a loud knock followed by "pastor?" from a deep voice on the other side of the door. Elijah, Tristan, and Brit jumped at the surprise of the knock. "Just another friend," the sheriff said while turning to open the door.

A tall, large-framed man dressed in a light gray police uniform entered the pastor's office. The sheriff hugged the man as he entered. "I've not seen you in years you crusty old S-O-B!" the man said as he squeezed the sheriff tight. "These are the kids?" the man said in his deep rumbly tone. The sheriff nodded in agreement, motioning the officer towards the group. "Hello guys, I'm Commander George Stinson with the Tennessee State Police," the man said as he extended his hand for a shake. "Well, it's nice to see another person with a gun," Brit said in her usual sarcastic tone while shaking the man's hand. But Brit meant what she said, the groups fear had grown uncontrollable and the appearance of another protector was a welcome sight. Hunter, and the thought of bringing justice to his killer, were the only things that kept the fearful three from fleeing Langford already. The State Policeman chuckled at Brits comment as he said, "if you're looking for guns, then you're in the right place," as he motioned towards a large black gun safe in the corner of the pastor's office.

"So, you think these are connected to Hunter somehow?" Tristan asked of Commander Stinson as he peered up at the law officer from behind a dark-brown folder containing a thick stack of police reports and photos. "I don't think, I know," the commander said in a deep firm voice. Commander Stinson was a man that was all business. After a brief exchange of pleasantries, he had explained to the group that he had been working similar cases out of Lanford for years. "People, well men especially, seem to have a way of disappearing in Langford," Commander Stinson said. "I've always had my own feelings and suspicions about the matter, but feeling are not facts," the lawman continued. Tristan exchanged the overflowing police folder with Elijah for the information that the pastor had provided. They sat silently reviewing the two folders as they all continued to listen to the commander. "All roads always seem to lead back to the Second Coming Bible Church," he said while shaking his head in disgust. "It always starts with someone disappearing without a trace. Sometimes they are reported and sometimes they're not. There's often some bull shit story passed around about how they up and left town for no good reason. The locals, along with the police, never give it a second thought and everyone goes about their business. But one thing is for certain, no one usually ever sees them again," Commander Stinson continued. "But over the years we have found a few bodies. Unfortunately, due to how long they have been missing, they haven't produced much useful evidence. The locals usually just assume it was an accident or a suicide," the commander said. "Hunter..." Brit muttered aloud. "Hunter," Sheriff Morales said in response to her.

"Your account, the discovery of the cell phone, along with Hunter's death clearly being a homicide, puts us closer than we have ever been," Commander Stinson said to the group of friends. "Plus, all of this other suspicious shit with Randy and the mountain of evidence that Pastor Bill has collected..." Sheriff Morales inserted quickly. "For a long time, Langford had a brick wall around it. But, with all the new blood like Sheriff Morales and Pastor Bill here, we have actually had the opportunity to investigate." The commander continued. "If this would have happened a few years back, back when the old sheriff was still alive, your friend would have been just another tragic young suicide." Commander Stinson Concluded. The sheriff, along with Commander Stinson, laid out their plan to the group. The newly discovered evidence would be enough to garner support for a search warrant for Ruby's home. Ruby's conversation with Granny Jean would be enough to search Grannies, Randy's, and

Seth's homes. From these four separate searches, the lawmen hoped to produce enough evidence to obtain further search warrants for the church, and other members of the congregation. The friends were to remain uninvolved and away from Ruby's place until the warrants could be executed. The trio of friends were shocked by how rapidly things were now unfolding. "Word travels fast in a small town, so we're going to execute the warrants simultaneously at 6:00 PM tonight," Sheriff Morales said. "I have a small group of officers from the state police on their way to Langford now to assist with the searches," inserted Commander Stinson. "We're not sure how much we can trust the sheriff's department, so we will not be including them other than Sheriff Morales," the commander concluded. It was then settled; the sheriff would drop the group of friends back off at Lake View where they would wait for the searches to take place.

Elijah's chair screamed a high-pitched moan as he nearly leapt from it. The young man emitted an audible gasp as the color appeared to drain from his flesh. He dropped the large, overfilled police folder on the floor of the pastor's office, feverishly pulled on the office door to open it, and ran into the hallway gasping for air. Elijah felt as if his heart was going to crawl out of his body; Elijah felt as if he were dying. Tristan and Brit quickly followed him in pursuit, only to find him slumped down in a corner, laying against the cool tile floor. "Elijah!" Brit shouted as she ran towards him. "Babe, what's wrong?" Tristan screamed in concern as he fell to his knees and slid across the slick shiny white floor to pull him into his arms. "Da, da, da, dad," Elijah softly stuttered as he tried to catch his breath. A circle of people had now formed around Elijah and the worried friends. "Dad," Elijah again softly said as he gasped for air. Everyone peered down at him in confusion; Elijah looked as if he had seen a ghost. "What is it babe," Tristan said as he kissed him on the forehead while pulling him closer. "It's my dad, he's in there" Elijah replied. "My dad is in that folder!" he then howled in distress.

As Elijah had been listening to the lawmen's plan, he had continued to pour through the stack of homicide and missing persons reports provided by Commander Stinson. Face after face, their haunting eyes stared back at him blankly. Eventually, Elijah found an all too familiar face in that stack of papers, he found a picture of his father. Initially, his mind could not make sense of what he was looking at. "Why would you be in here?" he had thought to himself as he gazed at the faded likeness of his father. He lifted the photograph from the page by pulling it from the paperclip that affixed it to a yellowing old police report. Behind the photo he found his father's name, his date of birth, and his social security number. His eye poured over the report, scanning up and down in a futile attempt to understand. His eyes eventually became transfixed on a word, a word that forced Elijah to depart completely from his known reality: *Missing*. The word caused Elijah to dig further into the pages of the stained and yellowing old report, eventually discovering a handwritten statement from his mother:

"It was a regular morning; I woke up around 6:30 AM and noticed that Henry wasn't in bed. I assumed that he was already up getting ready for work. I made my way into the kitchen to start a pot of coffee and I found a note next to the coffee maker. The note went on to explain how tired he was of our relationship, his fatherly duties, and how he couldn't take things anymore. The note said that he was leaving and to not look for him. It was signed – Henry. I then called my sister, Ruby Morgan, and she said he would probably

be back in a few days. She told me to wait and see if he turned up, but after a few days of waiting, I thought it would be best to report his disappearance. Some men from the church have been looking for him around town and I have called several of his friends, no one has seen or heard from him since his shift the day before at work. Things seemed fine when we went to bed that night, but we had been arguing a lot more over the last several months. I can't think of anyone that would want to harm him and I just couldn't imagine that he would ever hurt himself. I believe he just up and left; he walked out on his family. I just hope to find him for his sons' sake."

The statement was signed: *Victoria Morgan Howard.* Elijah read his mother's statement over and over; this was not the same story from his childhood. The farther he read, the more his confusion and panic grew. He quickly turned to the back of the report and read the reporting officers conclusions:

"The concerned wife believes that her husband walked out on her. All facts and evidence align with her initial report. After an extensive search of the surrounding areas and questioning of neighbors and coworkers, the subject in question is assumed to have simply chose to

no longer pursue a relationship with the wife and child. This is further corroborated by the statements of persons close to the subject in question in which he informed them that he planned to flee to either California or Florida. I see no current need to continue this investigation. This is based off of the statements provided and corroborating evidence."

Elijah flipped feverishly back and forth through the report; time seemed to stand still as he grappled with this bombshell. Neat and more modern appearing blue-ink notes littered the margins of the old report. Various items were circled, and others were underlined, lines were drawn leading to the thoughts of their author. "Missing" was circled with a line that led to a note that read: *"Presumed Deceased."* Ruby's name was underlined, along with his mothers, under each it read: *"Suspect."* A note directly beside of his mother's statement read: *"Fled to South Carolina with her young son after the disappearance."* Yet another piece of the puzzle emerged as Elijah continued to read the various notes: *"Conflicting the original report, more modern accounts of the man's disappearance state that he was killed in an industrial accident. The mill was shut down 20+ years ago and there is no way to corroborate this account. It's like the entire town has the same scripted story – fucking small town bull shit. Strangely similar to the other cases."* Elijah was crumbling inside as he started to piece together that everything he had known about his dad was a lie. What had happened to his father, why did his mother take him to South Carolina, and why would she lie to him? Elijah was struck with a revelation as if God himself had jolted him back to reality; it only made sense if the notes were true. The move to South Carolina, the lies of his mother, and the seemingly purposeful disconnection from any family or friends that might hold the truth, only made logical sense if his mother was somehow involved.

"Howard," Commander Stinson said as they each took their seat back in the pastor's office. After overcoming his panic attack, and a healthy dose of fresh air, Elijah was hungry for answers. "I didn't realize he was your father. I'm sorry I didn't put things together until now," the commander said apologetically. "What is all of this?" Elijah asked of him. As the commander sat silently trying to formulate the best way to break the news to him, Elijah went on to explain the story, the story that his mother had told him, to the commander. Commander Stinson patiently listened to Elijah for a few moments before cutting him off, "just stop, son," Commander Stinson said in his deep rumbling baritone voice. Brit grabbed Elijah's knee to stop the rhythmic tapping of his foot against the white tile floor; Tristan placed his arm around Elijah to comfort him. The three friends, along with Sheriff Jackson Morales and Pastor Bill, painfully listened to Commander Stinson reveal to them what he believed to be the truth.

"All roads lead back to the Second Coming Bible Church," the commander started. "All of those people in that folder were somehow connected to the church. Some seem like random passersby, but most were husbands of members of the congregation, people who spoke out actively against the church, those that the church would consider sinful, and the like," the loud booming voice of the commander said. "Your father was all three," Commander Stinson explained. "Your mother was born into the Second Coming Bible Church and became extremely active in it over the years, becoming that much more active after your birth. Henry, I mean your father," the commander said quickly correcting himself. "Your father was not pleased with the churches beliefs and felt as if he was losing her to what he feared was a religious cult."

Commander Stinson continued. "A fear that is now shown to be very well founded!" Pastor Bill Hall said in addition to the commander's comments. "Very well founded," the commander said in agreement with the pastor. "Your father wanted her to quit the church, he wanted to move you both away from Langford to escape the grip that the church had on the town," Commander Stinson continued. "There is some truth in that old police report, he did want to move to California or Florida, but he wanted to take you both with him," the commander explained. "As I was digging, I even found old job applications from where your father had been applying to different jobs in those areas," Commander Stinson said. "Your father was trying to save you and your mother from the church, but I believe his efforts ultimately cost him his life." Commander Stinson concluded.

Elijah leaned across his chair and balled up in Tristan's arms; Tristan had become Elijah's rock during what had become the worst time in his life. He broke down sobbing, soaking Tristan's t-shirt with his tears. Silence crippled the room as they each allowed him some time to process all that he had just heard; Elijah's random sniffle or gasp for air was all that one could hear. Pastor Bill quietly made his way behind Elijah and placed his hand on his shoulder, "God, help him?" the pastor whispered to God in the silence. Elijah was broken; all that the young man had ever known had just been clawed from him. Elijah's pain extended beyond his belief in Commander Stinson's words. The idea that his father had been taken from him, not by some industrial act of God or freak accident, but by the hands of his own flesh and blood crushed his soul. "Mom..." Elijah muttered as he finally broke his spell of silent weeping. He pulled himself up and sat up straight in his chair, wiping the tears from his swollen red eyes. "My mom?" he asked as he locked eye with Commander Stinson. "I believe she told her sister Ruby about your fathers plan to uproot the family and move y'all across the county," Commander Stinson responded. "The sisters approached the church with the problem, and the church provided a solution." He continued as Elijah was becoming visibly enraged at what he was hearing. "I believe your father was one of the first or not as well planned, they were sloppy and didn't think things through. This sloppiness caused your fathers disappearance to gain too much attention." The commander explained. "Your mother had to leave. If she left, the memory of you father would quickly fade."

He continued. Elijah's hands were now clinched into fists of anger; every morsal of truth only feeding his rage. "Son, your mother had to choose between Henry and the church, she chose the church." Commander Stinson concluded.

After what felt like hours in the belly of the Christ Almighty Worship Center, Elijah now knew the truth about his father. While he did not know exactly what had transpired, he knew enough to know that his mother and Aunt Ruby were at the heart of his father's disappearance and presumed demise. Elijah remained silent as Sheriff Morales dropped the trio of friends off at Lake View Park. With his pain-laden rage boiling over inside of him, he listened to Sheriff Morales again detail the plan for executing the search warrants. As the sheriff was recounting the specifics with the group, the ringing of his cell phone sharply interrupted him. The sheriff quickly answered with his usual "Sheriff Morales," followed by, "Ok, great! Right on time! I'll be there in 10 minutes." After placing the phone back in its appropriate place on his shiny-black leather duty belt, the Sheriff said victoriously, "We got it! We got the search warrants!" This was the first sliver of decent news any of them had received in a week. As happy as the news of the search warrant made the sheriff and Elijah's friends, it left him feeling worse. "What now?" Elijah thought to himself as he pondered the potential new scraps of truth that would be uncovered by the searches. "Just stay away from the church and stay away from Ruby's!" Sheriff Morales said as he swiftly made his way towards his shiny black *Impala*. "I'll call you soon!" he shouted as he slammed the car door and departed with its lights flashing and siren blaring.

"6:00 PM," Brit read aloud from her phone as the three stared out over the picturesque lake. "I wonder what's happening?" Tristan said in response to Brits statement. "Hopefully, they're catching whoever did this to Hunter," Brit snapped back. Elijah remained silent as he simply continued to stare into the lake's murky dark waters with his back to his friends. Brit approached him from behind, wrapping her arms around him in comfort and saying, "we'll figure it out, no matter what they find, we'll figure it out." This was the first moment since Elijah's awareness of the shocking truth that he felt at ease. His vengeful anger had since turned to the startling realization that, if all of this turned out to be true, he no longer had a family. As disconnected as he was from his roots, and as distant as his relationship with his mother had become, he took comfort in knowing that they were there. This comfort of knowing had quickly turned from a blessing to a curse. Tristan joined Brit in embracing Elijah; he openly wept. Elijah's tears were not cried in sadness or anger. In this isolated moment, Elijah wept tears of happiness. For a brief uninterrupted moment, while surrounded by his boyfriend and best friend, Elijah realized what he had remaining. Elijah had Tristan and Brit; they were all that he had left and all that he needed. Though, the pain of losing his family broke him, his friends love overflowingly filled the void his family left behind.

A violent roar pierced the tranquil sounds of crickets and other late evening critters that called the lake home. The sun had just set over Lake View Park and the friends were awaiting news from Sheriff Jackson Morales. Dim yellow headlights appeared at the parks gates and violently bounced up and down with a loud bang as the vehicle careened through the series of potholes at the parks entrance. "What the fuck?" Elijah said as he turned to see what was happening. Soon an older model white, rust speckled truck swiftly screeched to halt behind Tristan's SUV. Armed with shotguns, Seth Nelson and Randy Ward leapt from the truck and confronted the group of friends. "You couldn't just leave good enough alone, huh?" Seth shouted at them. "Get on the fucking ground!" Randy called out to the group. As Elijah, Tristan, and Brit complied with the armed and angry men, Randy quickly approached them. He zip-tied their hands behind their backs and instructed them to not move. Now defenseless, Randy Ward could feed his thirst for violence without fear that it would be countered. Seth chuckled as randy delivered blow after blow to Brits ribs with his steel toed work boots. Brit screamed out in pain as Elijah and Tristan wrestled with their bindings. "Nope!" Seth shouted with a chuckle as he pressed the cold steel barrel of the shotgun against Tristan's head. Randy then went down the line, beating each of them into unconsciousness. "We're going for a little ride," Randy said as he threw them one-by-one into the back of Tristan's SUV. After a moment of searching the three for the keys, they were off. Seth Nelson followed closely behind in his beat-up old truck.

Elijah wrestled with himself to maintain his consciousness as the three bounced around like loose groceries in the cargo hatch of the SUV. He could see the dim glow of the lights and could hear the loud puttering and squealing brakes of Seth's truck following closely behind them. It had all happened so fast that Elijah could not really comprehend what was going on. He faded in and out of consciousness; his body silently screaming out in pain each time he would come to. He whispered out to Tristan, and then to Brit. Neither responded and he feared that Randy Ward, in his fit of holy rage, had killed them. Elijah then heard a muffled "Bzzz-bzzz-bzzz-bzzz" from the front of the big SUV. "Hello," Randy Ward answered sharply. "Yeah, we found them out at the park. We're on our way there now." Randy then said before ending the call and shoving the phone back into his back pocket. Elijah again attempted to roust his boyfriend, lightly kneeing Tristan in his side. Tristan emitted a low guttural groan; he was still alive. No matter how hard he tried, Elijah was fighting a losing battle to maintain his consciousness and would soon succumb to his beating.

As he laid there staring up at the light-grey headliner of Tristan's SUV, the yellowish glow of Seth Nelson's headlights grew darker and darker. The road noise and random squeaks and rattles of Seth's old truck devolved into a singular hollow ringing; Elijah's eyes closed, and his body went limp.

In his mind, Elijah found himself transported back to South Carolina. He was standing on the sidewalk in front of his childhood home, observing where he had spent the years of his youth. Elijah had not spent much time in Big Rock, South Carolina since his move to Nashville; he had parted ways with the little town years ago. Elijah, becoming more aware of the fact that he did not fit in within the little town, had fled Big Rock and its beliefs with no intentions of ever looking back. As he stood there in his dream state, he examined every inch of the small white house. He noted that every detail was in order; things were just as he remembered. He could see the still cracked front window, the one that he had hit with a baseball when he was 12 years old. He could smell the fresh cut front yard, the same yard that he had mowed every Saturday. He could see the handful of bright- white rocking chairs that graced the homes large front porch, the same chairs where he had forced himself to kiss his first girl. Everything was just as he had left it. He soon felt a familiar presence behind him, followed by a warm and strong embrace. "Are you ready babe?" Tristan asked as he nuzzled his face into Elijah's neck with his arms wrapped tightly around him from behind. Elijah could feel Tristan's light stubble scratching softly against his skin; he could smell his lover's usual masculine fragrance. "I'm excited to meet your mom," Tristan then said as he patted Elijah on the bottom to motion him towards the door. As the couple slowly walked towards the front door, Elijah's reminiscent happiness was replaced with sheer terror. As the front door slowly started to open, it groaned loudly just as Elijah remembered. From the looming darkness behind the door frame stepped Ruby Morgan.

Upon seeing Ruby, Elijah was plunged instantly back into his now familiar nightmare. He was calling out to Hunter, screaming hopelessly into the black void. He then found himself again in the woods surrounding Lake View, wandering through the dense green forest aimlessly. Elijah once more chased Ruby to the water's edge, she again retrieved Hunter's slippery bloated corpse from the water's depths, and she again screamed out to him a verse from the bible. As Elijah laid unconscious and helpless in the back of the SUV, these nightmares repetitively played through his head. A big "thump" from the road snapped him momentarily back into consciousness, breaking the cycle of terror. Elijah quickly faded back to sleep and again found himself dreaming. The little white house from his childhood laid before him yet again; every miniscule detail was in order just as he remembered. Elijah's mind flashed back and forth between his childhood home and vivid images of his future. He could see living with Tristan, but the house would soon flash back into his mind. He could see Tristan proposing marriage to him, then he would be back in front of that little old white house. He could hear Brit's giddy "Yes, duh!" as he asked her to be his "best man," but the house would always cut his small moments of joy short. Elijah then found himself sitting on a porch swing, holding hands tightly with Tristan. As he peered down at their hands, they were noticeably wrinkled and aged. Elijah glanced up at a now old and feeble Tristan Rivera. "I love you Elijah Rivera," Tristan said in his now raspy aged voice. "I love you," Elijah replied as he laid his head against Tristan shoulder and closed his eyes. Elijah was again in front of the little white house in which he was raised;

he stood on the sidewalk clutching a bright-red plastic gas can. Flames poured from the homes roof, thick black smoke rolled from the house's windows and doors, and the house screamed in pain as it began collapsing in upon itself. Elijah could feel the fires glowing heat against his face as he watched his childhood home crumble into the earth.

"Just wait on the pastor," Elijah heard as he lifted his head to see where he was. His blurry vision slowly focused to reveal Seth Nelson and Rady Ward; Elijah found himself in what appeared to be a basement. He quietly began to observe his surroundings as he listened for clues as to what was happening. "We just do what we're told, you got that?" Randy said to Seth while poking him sharply in the chest. "I know, but did you really have to hurt them like that?" Seth asked of Randy with concern. "I just do what God says," Randy shouted back angrily. "Two faggots and a loudmouthed bitch! They need a little sense beat into them!" Randy screamed as his anger grew more and more. Seth defeatedly lowered his head in compliance with Randy. Seth Nelson was much more like Elijah Howard than he could ever admit; his attempts to be close to Elijah were of a personal nature long before they had become official church business. While Elijah had fled his small-town prison and eventually embraced who he knew himself to be, Seth had done the opposite. As Elijah had ran to Nashville seeking acceptance, Seth ran into the arms of the Second Coming Bible Church seeking forgiveness. Seth Nelson became entrenched in the church's teaching and fiercely loyal to its cause. Much like Elijah, Seth had learned how to hide himself well. But Elijah Howard's appearance in Lanford, awakened things in him that he thought were long dead. "The pastor will be here soon," Randy Ward muttered to Seth before saying, "Just stick to the plan."

The basement was an expansive, dimly lit open space. Elijah was tightly zip-tied to a beige metal folding chair in the center of the room; Tristan and Brit were bound and gagged next to him. Elijah could see old wooden crosses and various other religious relics scattered across the space. As he continued to scan the room to get his bearings, he noticed a large hand-painted plywood sign leaned against the wall ahead of him. It read: *The Second Coming Bible Church – Easter Service 9:00 AM to Noon.* They had been brought to the church. "Blessed be to God!" Elijah then heard a familiar voice say as another person entered the room;

it was Pastor Jacob Eldridge. After a few minutes of back and forth between the three men, the pastor appeared in front of the group of friends. Seth and Randy pushed at Brit and Tristan to wake them, resorting to slaps and punches when they did not come to rapidly enough. Brit and Tristan both cried muffled screams of pain through their cloth gags as they awakened confused and ailing from their previous beatings. "Welcome back Elijah, we're glad to have you!" Pastor Eldridge said to him enthusiastically. "I'm so glad we finally convinced your friends here to tag along as well!" he continued. From behind them, Randy Ward chuckled at the pastor's comments. "It's high time you gain an understanding Elijah," the charismatic pastor said. "It's time you learn your destiny, its time you all learn your purpose!" he continued, sounding as if he were preaching a Sunday sermon to his flock.

"You were born for this Elijah," Pastor Jacob Eldridge said. "God, and the church, had this planned for you long before you were called back to Langford," the pastor continued. "It's quite literally in your blood," the pastor said as he leaned down and whispered in Elijah's ear. Pastor Jacob Eldridge proceeded to explain to Elijah the details of "why?" he had so longed for since the beginning of the friend's horrific experience in Langford. He went on to tell Elijah that at his birth, the deacons of the church prophesied that he was chosen. Going into further detail, he explained that the Second Coming Bible Church's minister had always been of Morgan blood. He told Elijah about his namesake, the biblical prophet Elijah, and that the young man himself was born to prophesy to the church. Elijah was not only meant to be a prophet, but he was meant to help the church bring about Christ's second coming. Confused, Elijah stared back at the Pastor's nonsensical apocalyptic rantings about prophecies and bloodlines. "Let me be a little clearer Elijah," Pastor Jacob said. "Each Morgan that has led this congregation, has brought us one step closer to bringing about the seconding coming," he began as he knelt to lock eyes with Elijah. "My Grandfather, my father, me, and now you..." he continued as he gazed deeply into Elijah's soul. "I have done all that I can do. I have cleansed this foul world of as much evil as I can! It's your turn Elijah! You are the final step to the second coming," he explained. "You will lead us into the holy land," the pastor concluded. Bloodied and in shock, Elijah struggled to connect the dots as the pastor departed from his sight. "Watch them," the pastor said firmly to Seth and Randy as he left the room.

"Someone must have tipped them off," a uniformed state policeman shouted after an initial sweep of the house. Unbeknownst to the small trustworthy group of lawmen, one of the local judges had ties to Deputy Randy Ward and had given him a heads up. Word travels fast in a small town like Lanford, but not fast enough to grant the churchgoers enough time to hide their vicious crimes. "I fucking knew it!" Commander Stinson exclaimed in a victorious shout. While digging through the old Morgan homestead, they had unearthed a small mountain of evidence relating to the crimes of Ruby, the Second Coming Bible Church, and its parishioners. They had found church literature detailing "God's plan" for bringing about Christ's apocalyptic rage upon the earth, a list explaining each member's roles and how they fit within the church's hierarchy, and various mementos of missing persons. The dated manifesto-like plans explicitly detailed God's desire for the church to cleanse the world of *"non-believers"* and *"sinful individuals"* in ritualistic sacrifices to please their god. *"Whoever would not seek the Lord, the God of Israel, should be put to death,"* the manuscript repeatedly stated. At Randy Ward's, the police unearthed a more gruesome scene. In a small, half hidden crawlspace in Randy's basement, they discovered numerous bodies in varied states of decomposition. From dried fragments of bones to others that still had rotting flesh clinging to them, they discovered nearly twenty sets of remains. At Seth Nelson's place they found Hunter's ATM card, Seth's torn flannel shirt Elijah had spotted in the restaurant, other clothes that were speckled with brownish dried blood, knives covered in a similar appearing substance, and another copy of the churches sacred plan. The findings at Granny Jean's home were similar to those at Ruby Morgan's. The search led to the discovery of small mementos of those that had been sacrificed in the lord's name, and a more up-to-date copy of the manifesto. The cover of the roughly put together text bore a large black cross, and simply read: *In His Name*. While thumbing through the rambling text, Sheriff Jackson Morales discovered the truth about the church's plan for Elijah. He swiftly pulled his cell phone from his shined-black leather duty belt and frantically called Elijah. Call after call, Elijah did not answer the Sheriff's attempts to reach him. He raced from Granny Jean's to meet Commander Stinson at Ruby's; the commander had just made the same startling discovery. The pair of lawmen raced to Lake View park, only to discover that the friends were nowhere to be found.

    Still dazed and only half conscious, Elijah felt a warm pair of arms embrace him. "Wake up, dear," he heard his aunts familiar voice whisper in his ear. Elijah, pulling himself from his half-awake state, looked up to find his Aunt Ruby gazing down upon him with a loving stare. "Do you understand Elijah?" she asked, referencing the conversation he had with Pastor Eldridge. Shaking off his dazed state, Elijah replied, "What's going on Aunt Ruby? What is this?" After momentarily gathering her thoughts, Aunt Ruby said, "It's your turn Elijah," followed by a loving smile. "My grandfather, my father, my brother, and now you… it's finally your turn. We can finally bring about his second coming, we can finally fulfill his word, only you can fulfill the prophecy," Aunt Ruby continued. In stunned disbelief, Elijah quietly said, "Brother?" Elijah's mother, Victoria Morgan Howard, had only one sibling – Ruby Morgan. "Yes dear, your uncle," she said as she started to reply to his confusion. "Pastor Jacob is our brother, he is your uncle," the frail dying woman explained. "Just like you, he was sent away. When it was his time to lead, he was called back to Lanford to fulfill his part of the prophecy," she continued. "God did not bestow upon him the same blessing that he did you; his mother could not accompany him on his journey into the wilderness. Jacob was adopted by a family in Georgia that raised him in a church with similar beliefs to ours," Aunt Ruby explained, going into deeper detail on the churches process of ascension into the pastorship. Still hungry for answers, Elijah pressed his aunt for information. "Those people, my dad, mom?" he said as he started to give way to his emotions. "Whoever would not seek the Lord, the God of Israel, should be put to death," she said in response. "Those people are not like us Elijah! They are filthy and represent all that plagues this world!" Ruby said nearly screaming. "Your sorry excuse for a father was the worst of them all! Not only was he a sinner, but he wanted to pull you and your mother into his wicked and blasphemous ways, too!" she said with noticeable seething hatred for Henry Howard. "But even those that we despise, serves a purpose for our lord god," she said while calming herself. "Your mother was asked to make a choice, Elijah. Your mother chose God." Ruby said. "Though far away, your mother is as much of a part of this church as I am, as you will soon be." Aunt Ruby concluded.

"Let me ask you Elijah, do you dream?" Aunt Ruby asked. "Do your dreams seem to come True, Elijah?" she continued. The memories of his hellacious nightmares flooded his mind; the visions that had now all been proven true. Elijah pondered on the validity of his visions as he remained silently listening to his Aunt Ruby. "It's a gift from God," she continued. "Just let us go Aunt Ruby, please!" Elijah shouted back at the old woman. Elijah worried for Tristan and Brit as they slumped unconscious in their chairs, their bindings being the only thing holding them semi-upright. "Let us go!" Elijah shouted once more as he looked side to side, trying to check on his friend's wellbeing. "It's all part of God's plan, Elijah," Aunt Ruby calmly said to him as she placed her hand on his shoulder and quietly prayed. Elijah bounced and kicked as he wrestled with the zip-ties that were binding him to his chair. "You can't fight God, you can't resist the prophecy, Elijah," she shouted at him while praying more feverishly over him. Elijah quickly realized that he was no match for the zip-ties; brute strength would not save him or his friends from God's holy plan. "Then what Aunt Ruby?

What happens now? What about Tristan and Brit?" he shouted back at his praying aunt in frustration. Aunt Ruby removed her praying hands from him and took a step back; the frail dying woman stood there staring down upon him quietly for minutes. "You must give up your sins Elijah, you must be made pure," said Aunt Ruby decisively. "Your sins, the same sins that we helped Seth overcome, must be made right," she continued. "God's forgiveness must be earned, it must be earned through actions that are taken in his name," Ruby explained. "Like your mother, and so many others of this flock, you must make a choice," Aunt Ruby said as she glanced at Tristan and Brit. "You must choose God or the world, you must choose to act in his name, or to sit idly by while the world destroys his name," she boldly stated. "You can choose to lead us to the second coming, or you can choose to die in your sins," Aunt Ruby continued. The frail woman shuffled her way behind Elijah; after a few moments of fighting with his bindings she cut him loose. As Elijah stood from his chair, Aunt Ruby said, "I know what you will choose Elijah, for it has been prophesied by the lord our God."

VIII

A large earth-trembling "BOOM" shook the old church house to its foundation. The violent quake was swiftly followed by a rapid exchange of gunfire overhead; yells and screams pierced the eerie quiet that had surrounded Elijah since his arrival to the basement of the Second Coming Bible Church. Aunt Ruby and Elijah stared at one another, both surprised by the sudden commotion overhead. The firefight showed no signs of slowing as shot after shot rang out in old church house. Elijah could hear the metallic patter of shell casings dropping to the floor, followed by the loud thud of bodies falling in their wake. Yells and screams were growing nearer as Brit came to with a loud and painful groan. "Elijah!" she shouted in search of her best friend. He quickly knelt down to comfort her. "Wh, wha, what's going on?" she asked as she tugged at her firmly affixed bindings. Elijah looked her over in concern, tending to her wounds the best that he could. Elijah stuttered in his response, "J, j, j, just hang in there, ok?" She peered up at him only that much more confused. "Brit, Shut your mouth! Just keep quiet!" Elijah said to her in a harsh whisper. The ringing gunshots grew closer and closer; Pastor Eldridge and Seth Nelson burst through the thick metal basement door and into the room. They were both drenched in sweat and blood, remnants of the war they had been fighting above. "The door!" Pastor Eldridge shouted to Seth in a strong commanding voice. Seth quickly shut and locked the heavy door, he then wedged one of the old wooden crosses between the handle and basements rough concrete floor. Aunt Ruby ran over to them, panicked by their appearance and their apparent state of distress. "Thank God!" she shouted once she realized they had not been injured. The blood was not their own, it was that of their fallen foe.

"Randy's dead," said Pastor Eldridge to Ruby in a somber tone. She gasped loudly and then began praying aloud for his soul and thanking God for his sacrifice. Seth stood guard at the door, blood-soaked and shaking from what he had just experienced. "What do we do, Pastor?" Seth shouted out in fear. "We can't hold them off forever," the tall young man continued. Elijah, watching the exchange across the room, now placed himself between his tied-up friends and the door. He was on edge as he watched and waited to see what would come next. "What the fuck do I do?" he thought to himself as panic filled his body. Still reeling from his beating, and facing two armed men, he would surely lose. Elijah then did something that even surprised himself, Elijah prayed. "God, I know that we haven't talked lately, I know we don't see eye-to-eye, and I know that you're probably just bull shit, but help?" he silently spoke in his mind. Elijah was trapped in the basement of the Second Coming Bible Church, the only way out was guarded by an armed fanatical pastor, Seth Nelson, and his Aunt Ruby. To make matters that much worse, what awaited him and his friends on the other side of that door?

"Elijah..." Tristan painfully called out in an attempt to find his love. "Elijah, where are you?" he asked as he started to come to from his severe beating.

Elijah heard his calls for him, but so did Pastor Eldridge. "Do not let them through that door Seth!" the pastor shouted. Seth quickly scurried to push a table in front of the door to aid the old wooden cross in keeping the door firmly shut. Pastor Eldridge made his way cautiously towards Elijah, stopping within a few feet of him. "We need you…" the pastor called out to Elijah. "This is why you were put on this earth Elijah! The second coming has begun!" Pastor Eldridge charismatically shouted. Elijah gazed at him as he thought quickly about what to do. Aunt Ruby made her way towards the two men to join in the exchange. "Were blood," Aunt Ruby inserted as she lovingly peered at Elijah. "Fulfill the prophecy Elijah and make our family whole again," the pastor said. "Your mother can join us soon, it's all according to God's plan," Pastor Eldridge continued. Elijah's thoughts ran wild as their words finally got to him. His family stood before the young man, and his friends behind him. "Mom," Elijah thought to himself as he tried to wrap him mind around it all. The pastor's words forced him to examine what a future with his family and the church might look like. In this moment of fear and weakness, Elijah longed for his mother, and he longed for a return to normalcy. "It's all part of God's plan, it is your destiny, it has been prophesized," Pastor Eldridge continued. His words snapped Elijah from his fever-dream of a life that would include his family or the church.

Elijah knew that all he was hearing were fanatical pseudo-Christian rantings. Even though they were his family, he could not construct a vision of a functional or happy life with them in his mind. Elijah was suddenly overcome with rage at the realization that he was looking at Hunter's murderers; he steamed with anger as they continued to try to persuade him to embrace his lineage and their outlandish beliefs. As Elijah nearly blacked out from his now uncontrollable anger, the war overhead raged on. "You must make your choice Elijah, it is time," Ruby said as she walked towards him. "You must choose," she said as she touched his shoulder to reassure him. The pastor cautiously approached him, not sure if his ministering had convinced the young man to lean into his destiny. Ruby, releasing Elijah's shoulder, turned towards Pastor Eldridge and extended her hand. As Ruby began loudly praying in tongues, Pastor Eldridge reached behind him and pulled out a well-worn nickel-plated *Colt 1911* pistol from the small of his back. He stared down at the deadly piece of steel momentarily, and then placed it in Ruby's hand. Grasping the pistol tightly, Ruby said, "this has been passed down from pastor to pastor, Morgan to Morgan, since the very beginning." Seth, hoping to witness the historic church tradition, turned from the door to watch. "It's finally time, the second coming has arrived," Aunt Ruby said as she extended the gun towards Elijah. Elijah briefly froze, thinking that Ruby might shoot him. But he quickly realized that she was handing him the gun; she was holding the weapon by it's barrel. He took the heavy pistol cautiously into his hands, it shiny metal was still warm from its contact with the pastor's skin. As he felt the heavy gun in his hands, he looked down to observe an inscription engraved into it. Down the barrel of the *Colt 1911*, it read: ...*In His Name*.

Aunt Ruby took Elijah by his hand and led him in front of his still bound lover, and his best friend. Pastor Eldridge and Seth Nelson watched excitedly, prepared to witness God's prophecy manifest before them. Aunt Ruby squared Elijah with his friends, then taking him by the wrist and extending his arm and the gun forward towards Tristan's head. "It's time to choose, it's time to fulfill God's word," she said to him softly by whispering into his ear. Tristan's fearful eye's locked with Elijah's, dazed and still confused as to what was happening. Sensing Elijah's hesitation, Aunt Ruby again quoted the word of God to Elijah, *"Whoever would not seek the Lord, the God of Israel, should be put to death,"* she said firmly. "Bring mercy upon them, cleanse them of their worldly sins, and fulfill the prophecy," Pastor Eldridge shouted out at Elijah. "Do it, Elijah. Do it in his name..." Ruby said to him in a calm motherly tone as she released his wrist. Elijah still shaking, battered, and bruised, stood in front of Tristan trembling with the gun to his head. Elijah's visions from his time in the back of Tristan's SUV again flashed before his mind's eye. He could again see living with Tristan in Nashville, he vividly witnessed Tristan's proposal to him, he again recalled Brit's giddy excitement over his offer to be his "best man," and he again was transported back to see himself and Tristan sharing a porch swing towards the end of their long life together. "Elijah?" Brit called out to him pulling him from his life-like visions. Elijah had indeed prophesized what was to come, it was nothing like what he had been told by Aunt Ruby and Pastor Eldridge.

As Aunt Ruby prayed louder and louder chanting in tongues, Elijah steadied the pistol to fulfill his prophecy. Two loud shots rang out, echoing sharply through the large concrete and cinderblock basement of the old church. "Fuck God!" Elijah shouted as Pastor Jacob collapsed with a "thud" against the rough concrete floor. Elijah, with near precision, shot the pastor twice in the forehead. The old *Colt's* .45 caliber rounds made quick work of Pastor Jacob Eldridge's brain, instantly blowing its bloody hate-filled thoughts against the wall behind him. Ruby shrieked loudly as Elijah turned the gun on Seth and instructed him to lay down his weapon. Seth, still shaking from his recent gunfight, quickly surrendered, and laid down his gun on the floor next to him. "Elijah, what have you done?" his Aunt Ruby shouted at him. "Why Elijah, why would you…" Seth started to say as he was quickly cutoff by Elijah. "Fuck you Seth!" Elijah shouted back at him, his rage now at a roaring boil. "W, w, we, we, can still fix this Elijah," Seth said in a stuttering futile attempt at persuading Elijah to follow God's plan, rather than his own. "You can still choose God," Seth screamed out.

God did not reside in the Second Coming Bible Church; Elijah was now certain that he never did. Seth

Nelson now grappled with the reality of what he was facing. Seth did not fear prison or death; the youth filled young man did not fear anything of this world. Seth Nelson, however, did fear the wrath of God. He could not allow God's prophecy to go unfulfilled; he was now the one forced into a position of choosing. Elijah, reminiscent of their initial friendship, somehow still had a soft spot for tall and goofy southern man. Elijah reasoned and pleaded with him to not fight back as he approached him. But Elijah's compassionate words fell on deaf ears; ear's that had been purposely deafened by the vile teachings of the Second Coming Bible Church. Seth screamed out in a holy rage, rushing quickly towards Elijah. Another loud "pop" rang out, followed by the metallic jingle of the .45 caliber cartridge bouncing against the concrete floor. Seth gasped loudly and clutched his chest as he slumped to the ground. Elijah carefully approached the young man as he lay in the floor, clawing at a gurgling dime-sized hole in his chest. As Elijah peered down at a dying Seth Nelson, he couldn't help but think that he had been a victim of this as well. He related deeply to the nearly dead man, seeing a version of himself in Seth's confused eyes. "That could have been me," Elijah thought silently as he watched Seth's gurgles and gasps for air grow more and more infrequent. In another world, in another life, if things had just been slightly different, Elijah could have easily found himself in Seth's shoes. After his few moments of somber "what ifs?" Elijah's compassion quickly turned back to rage. "Fuck you Seth Nelson," he shouted down at the corpse before turning to face his defeated Aunt Ruby. The ailing woman had now slumped down to the ground, an involuntary response to the events that were unfolding around her. Elijah loomed over the frail dying woman, enraged by the thoughts of what she had done to him and his friends. "You did this! You killed Hunter!" he shouted at her as he pulled her up by her thinning mop of black hair. With Ruby's hair in one hand and the pistol in the other, he pressed the barrel of the gun firmly against the woman's forehead. "Fuck you and fuck your God!" Elijah cried out.

Another boom shook the foundation of the old house of worship as Pastor Bill Hall and a group of heavily armed men broke down the door and stormed the basement. Pastor Bill Hall was more than a timid preacher; over the years he had built a sizeable network of militiamen to act as a counterforce against growing cult extremism. Pastor Hall had been preparing for years, just as the Second Coming Bible Church had been. But the old pastor had been preparing to stop the vile and hate filled actions of those that chose to use his God as an excuse to persecute the world. Quickly spotting Elijah preparing to execute Ruby, the pastor screamed out to him, "Elijah, don't do this son, this is not who you are!" Elijah was in a trancelike state as he stared vengefully down at his crying Aunt Ruby. "Do it Elijah!" the woman shouted up at him. "Do it! I've failed God!" she wailed as she called out to the heavens for forgiveness. Ruby Morgan did not call out to her God to forgive her for the lives she helped to cut short, she did not seek forgiveness for the pain that she had inflicted upon the world, nor did she beg God for mercy for any of the vile and evil acts she perpetrated in his name. Ruby Morgan begged of God to forgive her for not fulfilling his sacred prophecy. "I love you," Elijah heard a week voice say. He then turned to see both Brit and Tristan watching him as he prepared to extract his vengeful justice upon his Aunt Ruby. "Whatever happens Elijah, we'll figure it out. We always figure it out," Brit said in her now weak and raspy voice. Elijah dropped Ruby to the ground by releasing her hair and angrily said to her, "you don't deserve mercy," before dropping the gun and running to free his battered friends.

Pastor Bill Hall and his group of holy warriors ran to the trio's aid, the pastor's sharp knife easily sliced through the thick-black zip-ties that bound Brit and Tristan to their chairs. Ruby Morgan now found herself the one restrained, still pleading for God to have mercy on her soul as she laid against the cold rough concrete floor with several militiamen surrounding her. Pastor Bill and a handful of his men helped to get Tristan and Brit to their feet; Elijah wrapped his arm under Tristan to aid him in walking out of the church. The sweet-metallic smell of blood mixed with the burnt sulfurous smell of gunpowder and hung the humid and stale air of the old church house. The smell only grew that much more intense and nauseating as the friends slowly climbed their way up the stairs to the main church. Bodies of fallen militiamen and various members of the extreme church, were strewn across the large room. The pooling blood created dark puddles as it soaked into the thick red carpet of the Second Coming Bible Church. This was not the first blood the old church house had seen, but it was the most. The group made their way down the aisle and towards the door, the same aisle

Elijah and Seth had walked up just weeks prior. The numerous brass shell casings jingled under their feet, and the bloody carpet squished with every step they took. The faint wail of sirens erupted in the distance, breaking the silence of the now still and quiet church. As Sheriff Morales, Commander Stinson, and now, The Tennessee Bureau of Investigation screeched into the small parking lot, the group emerged from the unholy little church and into the cold night air. The now large group of lawmen were swiftly followed by a small army of fire and emergency medical personnel. A loud "wop, wop, wop," echoed from the sky as a blinding light poured over the group of survivors and their heroes from above. Elijah handed Tristan over to a paramedic and collapsed on to the steps of the Second Coming Bible Church.

A muffled "Beep, beep, beep, beep," filled the room as Elijah started to regain his consciousness. He gazed up into a flickering fluorescent light above him, trying to get his bearings and orientate himself to where he was. He pushed upwards against the crunchy, slippery mattress and scanned his body to find bruises, bandaged wounds, and an I.V. protruding from his arm. He then heard a familiar gruff voice say, "there he is."

It was Sheriff Jackson Morales; the calloused policeman was standing at the foot of Elijah's hospital bed. "Tristan, Brit?" Elijah shouted to the sheriff as he wrestled with the medical equipment attached to his body. "Woah, woah, woah," the sheriff said as he ran to Elijah's side to comfort him. "They're fine!" he said as he grabbed Elijah's arm. "Brit had some internal bleeding and is coming out of surgery now. They're stitching Tristan up as we speak," Sheriff Morales Explained, finally calming Elijah's concern for his friends. "Tristan will be in here any minute," the sheriff said as he smiled at Elijah. "You and Tristan are pretty tough guys," the sheriff continued. "But that Brit, she's a firecracker!" the sheriff said and laughed as he took another misguided attempt at humor. "Hell, she tried to fight me when I told her she needed to have surgery," the gruff sheriff said as he pointed to a small bruise on his cheek. "She's got a mean right hand," Sheriff Morales said laughingly as he explained his wound. Elijah, through his pain, finally cracked a smile at the old sheriff. After a quick laugh, the sheriffs face grew serious. "I need to update you about the case," Sheriff Morales then said in a more professional tone. "We have Ruby Morgan in custody, and she is being charged," the sheriff informed Elijah. Sensing that there was more, Elijah waited patiently for the sheriff to speak. "Officers in South Carolina have also taken your mother into custody. During the raid, a flashbang caused her home to catch fire. She was unharmed, but she'll be extradited back to Tennessee and will face similar charges to your aunts, including the murder of your father," the sheriff told Elijah in a somber tone. Elijah was not happy, nor was he sad, Elijah was simply done. He was done with the lies, betrayal, and evil that he now knew permeated his bloodline. If anything, Elijah was content in knowing that the remainder of his family would soon pay for their sins. He and the sheriff sat in silence for a few uninterrupted moments, processing all that had happened over the last week. "You saved them Elijah," the sheriff finally said. Elijah looked up at him with confusion, failing to remember all that had taken place just hours ago. "You saved your friends lives." Sheriff Morales said in a proud fatherly tone as he set down on the edge of Elijah's bed.

After giving statement after statement to various law enforcement officials, Elijah now found himself alone in his hospital room. He pulled off the various wires and tubes that were attached to his body, and he yanked the I.V. from his arm. Elijah could wait no longer, he had to see his friends. He groaned in agony as he rotated towards the edge of the bed, eventually pushing himself up and to his feet. He soon emerged from the dim room and into the bright white halls of the Lola Regional Medical Center. He was quickly greeted by a nurse that ran over to aid him. "My friends?" he asked of the kind faced nurse. "I've been waiting for you," the middle-aged woman replied. "Come on, lets go see them," she said as she wrapped her arm under Elijah and assisted him down the hallway. "He's right there," she said as she stopped him in front of a large wooden door. She then swung open the door to reveal a well beaten, but conscious Tristan Rivera. "Tristan!" Elijah shouted as he limped hurriedly towards Tristan's bed. "Elijah!" Tristan shouted in return as he forced himself up in his bed. Tristan shouted out in pain as Elijah leapt on top of him. "Ow! Ow! Ow! Babe!" Tristan shouted as he embraced Elijah. The kind nurse crept from the room, slowly closing the large wooden door behind her. The two laid there together, promising to never let go of each other again. After hours of tears and silently embracing one another, the door burst open with a loud "bang!" Tristan and Elijah, still jumpy from their hellacious night, jumped in fright of the loud noise. "Fucking wheelchair," they heard as they witnessed Brit trying to wheel herself into the room. "Sup, bitches?" she said as she fought her way through the door. "What? What are you looking at?" she said with a chuckle as she neared the bed. "Brit!" Elijah squealed as he ran to meet her.

The sun was setting over Nashville; the sky was on fire with vivid purples and reds. The fiery sunset poured through the tall winding trees that lined the luscious green field. Rows of chairs to the left and right were filled with hundreds of people, and a bright-white long carpet separated the rows of full seats. The light murmur of the gathered crowd quickly grew silent as Elijah appeared behind them with Brit on his arm. Elijah was striking in appearance; his breathtaking good looks were only compounded by his dark-blue fitted suit. Brit, standing beside of him in a flowing cream gown, squeezed his arm tightly and whispered, "are you ready?" Elijah gazed happily into her eyes and said, "more than ever." Elijah and Brit slowly started to make their way down the aisle and towards the flower covered arbor at the end. Beside the arbor stood a dapper Sheriff Jackson Morales in boxy oversized suit. The tough old lawman was smiling ear to ear and fighting a losing battle against weeping. Tristan stood under the arbors arch, wiping his tears on the sleeve of his suit jacket while he awaited the arrival of his groom. As Elijah met Tristan under the flowery arch, Brit joined Sheriff Morales, laying her head against his shoulder. Pastor Bill Hall presided over the marriage, reading from a small note card, as he had thought it best to leave his bible at home this day. After both men rushed through their vows, neither of them wanting to wait any longer to be married, they each sealed their bond with a prompt "I do!" and passionately kissed as the crowd cheered. "Get a room you horndogs!" Brit shouted as she clapped and screamed. As Elijah and Tristan warmly embraced each other, Elijah whispered into his new husbands' ear, "I'll never let you go again..." Elijah Howard was in fact a prophet, but not a prophet of the Second Coming Bible Church, nor was he a prophet of God. All that he had seen in his dreams somehow manifested into reality; his visions had proven true. But Elijah's visions coming true had nothing to do with Godly intervention; Elijah Howard made his choice, he acted on love, and along with his actions came more than he ever hoped for.

Made in the USA
Columbia, SC
18 March 2021